BILLIONAIRE'S PROMISE

L. STEELE

1

Ava

"I'm Baron." He glares down at me. "And you're in my way."

Baron? I blink, why is that name so familiar? "Do I know you?" I scowl, "And what do you mean that I am in your way? I almost fell—"

"Until you didn't," he points out. "I saved you from hurting yourself."

"I thought you were someone else." I take in his harsh features, the dark blonde hair that falls over his forehead, the rich tan of his skin which hints at a life spent outdoors, the dark eyelashes that fringe a pair of brilliant blue eyes. The kind of eyes you could drown in, get lost in. So deep that they hide secrets. Secrets which I have had enough of. I no longer want to be drawn into something I can't fathom. I yank at his grasp and he releases me so suddenly that I stumble back. He grips my shoulder, holds me long enough to ensure that I've found my balance, then releases me.

"You're better off without him." His lips twist.

"How do you know that?" A chill runs up my spine and I wrap my arms around myself.

"Anyone who has you running barefoot on the sidewalk at," he glances at the watch on his thick wrist, "six in the morning, clearly doesn't deserve you."

"And I suppose you do?" I purse my lips together. What the hell is wrong with me? Why am I baiting him? Why does he rub me the wrong way, and after he'd saved me from a bad fall? I could have hurt myself... Not that I could be hurt any worse, after how Edward had turned and left.

Edward. I swing around and stare at the now deserted road. The houses on either side of the quiet London street mock me. The fog that envelops the street clears, and for a second, I think I see him in the distance. I take a step forward, trip over the same crack in the pavement. Damn it! I stumble once more and when thick fingers wrap themselves around my wrist, I try to shake them off. "Let go of me," I huff.

"Why should I when, clearly, you can't put one foot in front of the other without hurting yourself?"

"*You're* hurting me now." I glance down at where his massive palm is curled around my hand. Warm tanned skin, scarred knuckles that lead up to a veined forearm, peppered with hair. The sheer masculinity of this man is overwhelming. I glance up again into those blue eyes. The scowl that laces his features, the grooves etched into his forehead hinting at his permanent dark mood.

He releases me, and I turn back toward the image I'd seen, but the road is empty. The early morning sun's rays slant down, and the fog seems to disperse in front of my eyes.

"He's gone," I mumble. "I couldn't stop him." A tear squeezes out from the corner of my eye and I slap it away angrily.

"No one's worth crying over."

"Oh?" I swallow down the ball of emotion that clogs my throat, then pivot and brush past him. "And how would you know that?"

"Because I spent a lot of my early years crying over something that could never be righted."

"You?" I pause, then stare at him across my shoulder. I tilt my head up, all the way up, to take in his massive height. He's as tall as Edward… No, taller. And his shoulders are broader. His massive chest hints at hours spent in some kind of physical work. Maybe he trains a lot? Or he's in some kind of profession that demands he stay in top condition? What do I care anyway? Edward is gone. He hadn't left behind even a note. He'd shagged me—okay, so I'd asked him to shag me, fine, not denying that—and then he'd left.

He'd crept away while I was asleep, after promising we'd be together, and now I am never going to see him again. My stomach twists, my guts churn, and the bile rolls up my throat. Goddam it. I spring to the side, fall to my knees, and am violently sick. I retch so hard, tears run from my eyes again, my hair falls over my face, and then he's there. He piles my hair on top of my head, holds my forehead while I empty my guts out. Somebody, kill me. This has to be the worst day of my life. Getting sick, and because that's not bad enough, in front of a stranger.

When I am done, he offers me his handkerchief. I glance up at him, and he jerks his chin, "Take it."

When I don't reach for it, he pats my mouth with the fabric. I snatch it from him, turn my face away and dab at my lips. I rise up, and he's with me. I turn and am about to hand the cloth back to him, then grimace and stuff it in the back pocket of my jeans. "I'll wash it and give it back to you."

I turn away, take a step forward and my legs seem to turn to jelly. Fuck me, what the hell is wrong with me? The ground comes up to meet me again, and this time, I am not surprised when he scoops me up.

"Put me down," I mumble.

He doesn't reply. Instead, he begins to walk back the way I'd come. "Which house?" he asks, his tone brusque.

"That one." I point toward the first house on our right.

He walks toward it, up the garden path, then takes the stairs two at a time, as if he isn't carrying me. Not that I weigh much, but hey, he could, at least, be out of breath or something. But there's not a hitch or any change in his breathing pattern to indicate that he is carrying the weight of another person. He stops at my front door.

I reach into my front pocket, pull out my keys. He shifts my weight, takes the key from me, unlocks the door, then walks through, before crossing the floor to the settee where he deposits me. He straightens then points a finger at me. "Stay there."

"Not that I was going anywhere, but seriously, what the hell is your problem?" I huff. "And I didn't give you permission to come into my house." I frown.

He arches an eyebrow, trains those piercing blue eyes on me, and I subside.

He places the keys on the coffee table then pivots and walks toward my kitchen as if he owns the place. Shit, the way his massive frame takes up space, he does, actually. His physical presence seems to absorb all of the oxygen in the space and my lungs burn.

Or maybe that's because of the growing realization that I've lost him. I've lost Edward. Had I ever had him? And he never told me that he isn't returning, but the sick sensation at the bottom of my stomach insists that he won't be anytime soon. My palms sweat and my chest hurts. I sit up and the world swims around me again.

"I told you to stay put," he chides as he appears from the direction of the kitchen. He squats down in front of me, handing me a glass of water.

I take it and drink from it, upturn the glass, but he grips my wrist. "Not too much or it'll make you sick again."

I lower it, glance through my eyelashes at him. He takes the glass from me, places it on the table.

"How are you feeling now?" He searches my face.

"Better," I mutter. "I need to brush my teeth."

He peruses my features then nods, rises to his feet, and scoops me up with him.

"I can walk," I protest.

He simply stalks into the bedroom, putting me down at the entrance to the bath.

I step inside, turn to shut the door to find him standing, hands folded, a stillness about him that is at odds with just how alert his eyes are.

"You can go," I mumble, "I'll be fine."

He doesn't move. Not so much as blinks an eye.

"Whatever." I sigh, then close the door and lock it. Not that I don't trust him. Okay, I don't trust him. So what if he saved me from hurting myself, then hauled me back in here and made sure I was hydrated? I'd trusted Edward and what did he do…? He broke his vows for me. He fucked me. OMG, he took my virginity and then left me. He's not coming back, and once more, I've screwed up my life.

I had gone after the impossible. He'd been a priest, for hell's sake. Why did I have to fall for him? Why had I been so attracted to him that I couldn't conceivably want anyone else but him? Of course. Not only had I spoiled my career by leaving behind the safety of a degree and a possible nine-to-five job, but then I also had to go after a completely unsuitable man. Typical Eve.

Eve. Now I'm calling myself Eve? My heart seems to shatter. I crumple to the floor, hide my face in my hands and begin to weep. Large sobs that hurt my chest, fill my throat, and overflow until I am sure I am going to shatter into a million pieces, and every one of them would still cry, *Edward. Get over the dramarama, bitch.* Clearly, I've been reading too many romance novels if I am becoming so over-the-top sentimental. But damn him, he broke my heart.

In such a short period of time, he'd crawled under my skin, and imprinted himself into my soul in a way… A way that only a man of God could have. Someone who was in service of a higher purpose than himself. Shit, what am I thinking? Why am I making excuses for him, when all he's done since I met him is give me second place in his life? He may have broken his vows for me, but then he left, and I simply cannot fathom why. Hell, maybe it wasn't even for me that he broke his vows. I may not know what happened, but clearly, there was something bothering him when he got here.

More tears well up and my pulse thuds at my temples. A banging sound fills my head and I am sure it is my heart pounding in my ears, but then a male voice calls behind me, "Open up, or I swear, I am going to break down this door."

"Shit. Shit. Shit. Shit." I scramble up, grab hold of a hand towel and wipe my face with it.

The banging increases in urgency, then the sound of a shoulder crashing against the bathroom door reaches me.

"Stop," I yelp as I rush toward it. The last thing I need is for the door to be broken down. The bloody landlord would definitely take it out of my deposit. I reach the doorway, yank it open and come face to face with Mr. Grumpy Pants himself.

"What's your problem?" I snap.

"You," he looks me up and down, "you're my problem."

"Jesus." I gape at him. "You insult me in my own home? If you hadn't helped me earlier—which, by the way, wasn't required. I can take care of myself, but you did and I am grateful for it, but now you can leave."

"No."

"What?"

"I'm not going anywhere," he informs me. "Not until you have a shower and get a good breakfast. You need it after your crying jag."

"Crying jag." I flush. Of course, he heard me weeping my stupid heart out. Why the hell does he care how I feel? Why is he so concerned about me? "Who the hell are you anyway?" I scowl. "You're seriously giving me the creeps, the way you've barged into my life."

"And you are getting antsy for no reason." He holds up his arms. "You can pat me down if you want. You'll see I'm not dangerous."

Dangerous? He doesn't need weapons to be dangerous.

I look him up and down. "No, thank you, and by the way, I am taken."

"Taken?"

I nod. "My uh…man… He just left earlier."

"That's who you were chasing after?"

"Only because he forgot his phone," I lie.

"He forgot his phone..." he says slowly.

"Y…yeah." I swallow.

"So, you were chasing after him, barefooted?"

I nod.

"So, where's his phone?"

"None of your business." I scowl. "Will you please step away now so I can shower?"

"Not stopping you."

Anger twists my guts and it feels good. Good to be able to focus on something else, other than that jerk-hole who walked out of my life. How dare he play with me like this? How dare he stalk in here, claim me, imprint himself all over me, then walk out without looking back once? How dare he?

I fist my hands at my sides, then step back and slam the door shut. I lock it again, march over to the shower and turn it on. I shed my clothes, step under the hot water and allow it to flow over me. A few hours ago, he'd stood here as I had sucked him off. Hell. Hell. Hell. No need to figure out if I will be going to hell for having teased the Father into breaking his vows… Clearly, I am already there.

Is this my punishment from the other One in our relationship? The One Above. The Almighty who, no doubt, is displeased with me for having tempted one of His own to sin. Gah, stop that. Why are you questioning things as if the Father's influence has rubbed off on you? Not long ago, he'd been here rubbing off on me. Ugh. Stop that. He's gone, remember?

He left you.

Walked out without a backward glance. So why are you still so… so…hung up on him?

I raise my head toward the spray, let the hot water wash away the tears. I stand under the pelting drops until my head clears somewhat. Then switch it off and dry myself. I wrap the towel around myself, secure it and walk into the bedroom. It's empty. Of course, it would be. Why had I thought otherwise? I walk over to my closet, pull on my underclothes, a pair of leggings and a sweatshirt.

I need to stop holding onto hope that he'll return to me. There's no reason to think he will. His actions had all been intended to hurt. Clearly, he wants me to forget about him. Except, he took my virginity, something I'll never forget. To be fair, I hadn't mentioned to him that I was a virgin. Thank God for that. I got to spend some time with him. *Yeah, and he broke your heart too, how about that, hmm?*

It's only your heart... It will mend... Unlike whatever he is facing. It has to be something catastrophic that propelled Edward to leave behind the priesthood and take off. Something I intend to get to the bottom of.

I grab a hair tie, pile my hair on top of my head, then walk out of the bedroom, across the living room toward the kitchen.

The scent of toast and coffee reaches me. My stomach growls. I step inside the kitchen, pause. His back is to me and his broad shoulders are framed against the first rays of the sun that pour in. They halo him, highlight him, make him seem larger than life. A behemoth. Someone who came into my life, for what? To save me? From Edward? From myself? A shiver runs down my spine. I shake my head, walk over to the coffee pot to pour myself a cup. He turns to me then. "Sit." He jerks his head toward the table. "I'll pour it for you."

"But—"

"Go on," he says, his voice impatient. "This will go much faster if you cooperate."

I blink. "Excuse me?"

"I mean," he schools his features into an expression of patience, "sit down, please."

I hesitate. That *please?* It didn't sound like he meant it. In fact, it sounded as if he'd said it with much reluctance. He raises an eyebrow, turns his gaze to the table then back at me.

Fine, be like that. I slap the mug back on the kitchen counter, stomp over to the table and seat myself. I play with the ends of my hair, pull off the band and place it on the table. Then drum my fingers on the table. He turns, surveys my restless fingers, and I cease the movement instantly. Goosebumps flare on my skin. What is it about his glare that makes me want to rush to obey him?

He pours me a cup of coffee, brings it over, along with a stack of pancakes on a plate. On a second plate he's piled hash browns, baked beans and toast, which he places between us.

I blink down at the two plates, then up at him. "Uh, who is all this for?"

"You." He turns to grab his own plate, then sits opposite me. "I substituted flaxseeds for the eggs for the pancakes," he remarks.

I glance at him. "You did?"

He nods.

"How do you know that I am vegetarian?"

"Because you don't keep any meat or fish or eggs at home?"

Right. "I do eat milk and eggs," I mutter. "Just happen to be out of them..." I shuffle my feet, "the eggs, I mean." Gah, shut up, what's wrong with me? Why do I tend to babble in his presence? Why does he make me nervous?

He picks up his fork and knife, then eyes me across the table. "You're not eating," he admonishes.

"Neither are you."

His lips quirk, then he glances down and digs into his food.

I follow his lead, manage to make my way through a quarter of the pancakes, before I give up and lean back. I watch him demolish the food on his plate like he hasn't eaten in years.

When he glances up, I push my half-filled plate toward him.

He scowls at it. "You haven't eaten nearly enough."

"It's enough," I insist.

"It's enough when I say it is."

I blink at him, "Seriously, you didn't just say that."

"What's wrong with what I said?"

"Are you trying to be funny or something?"

"I've never been more serious." He leans forward, "You need your energy; you are wasting away."

I scoff. "I wouldn't call this," I point at myself, "wasting away."

"You're right."

"I am?"

He nods. "You have decent curves. I've seen better, of course, but you'll do."

I gape at him. "You...you're...something, you know that?"

"I often have that effect on women."

I jump to my feet. "Out. Get out."

He meets my gaze with a cool glance. "You're overreacting."

"And you're not welcome here anymore."

"I'm afraid that's not your call to make."

"What?" I frown. "This is my apartment and you are seated at my table—"

"In front of a breakfast I cooked for you."

"A breakfast you can shove up your—"

He tilts his head, and there's just enough warning in that single glance for me to press my lips together. Why the hell had I allowed him, a complete stranger, into my home? And yet, why does that jut of his jaw, the spark of anger in his eyes, feel so…right?

No, no, no. This can't be happening. I just had one man walk out on me a few hours ago, and already, I am attracted to another? Talk about being a slut. Only I'm not one. Hell, I'd never wanted to sleep with anyone else before Edward. And now, suddenly, here's another man, someone to whom I am attracted just as much? With as much intensity as Ed… It's the same... Yet different, though. With Ed…the pull had been sharp, incisive, almost clinical in the precision with which my heart had gravitated toward him. Probably because once I'd realized that he was a priest, every single interaction with him had felt wrong...but with Baron…there's a freedom. A need… An overwhelming pull to throw myself at him, throw myself at his mercy, and beg him to do anything he wants with me. Maybe the need Edward ignited opened up a hotbed of something… Some nameless emotion, some twisting sensation that I had hidden away for too long. And now it's out there, and I feel like I am exposed and aching and throbbing and crying out for attention.

My chest tightens. My scalp tingles. My skin suddenly feels too tight for my body. I take a breath and my lungs burn. My knees knock together and I sit down in the chair so suddenly that the legs creak.

"You okay?" His gaze intensifies as he peruses my features and I look away.

Heat flushes my skin and my toes curl. My own thoughts have

aroused me in a way that I never would have expected. My thighs clench and my center throbs. The soreness in my backside and between my legs pulses and writhes. Shit, what's wrong with me? I place my elbows on the table, bury my face in my hands.

I sense him move then. Hear his chair scrape as he pushes it back. The pad of his footsteps, the sound of a glass being filled with water. His footsteps approach, then I hear the thunk of the glass hitting the table in front of me.

"Drink," he commands.

I stiffen. What the hell is his problem?

"Do it," he insists.

I lower my hands and scowl at him.

He simply folds his arms across his chest and glares at me.

Jerk.

I glower back, and his gaze simply intensifies. Hot, burning, overwhelming. The flesh between my legs throbs. Heat flushes my cheeks. I glance away, take a sip. And does the man move away? Of course, not. He waits until I tilt the glass and drink half its contents.

Satisfied, he sits down, pushes my untouched coffee mug toward me.

I reach for it, take a sip. The bitter taste of the java blooms on my palate. I sigh out my appreciation, take another sip. Dark, rich notes of chocolate, laced with a sweeter taste of honey, and in between, the characteristic bitterness of coffee flickers across my tongue. "It's good." I blink up at him. "Which coffee grinds did you use?"

"The one you had in your coffee canister?"

"Oh." I glance down at the cup, take another sip. "You sure?"

"Yeah."

There's an amused edge to his tone. I glance up to find his lips twitch.

"No need to make a national joke out of my question," I mutter. "It's simply that the coffee tastes so much better than when I make it."

"It happens." He raises his shoulders. "When someone else cooks the same dish you do, they have a different touch, a unique way of assembling the ingredients, which will, therefore, be perceived differently by your taste receptors."

"Oh." I blink. "Are you a chef?"

His features close. "No."

He gets up, takes both our plates and the used cutlery over to the sink and begins to wash up.

"I can do—"

He glares at me over his shoulder, and I shut up. Of course, Mr. Growly Pants will do what he wants, when he wants. He finishes the washing up—returns for my now empty coffee cup—which he takes to the sink along with his, and washes that up too. He finishes drying them, puts them away—in the correct places on the shelves, then wipes the counter clean.

"Make yourself at home," I bite out. "In fact, why don't you move in, while you're at it?"

He pauses, then turns to me. "Not yet."

My jaw drops. "What do you mean, not yet? I don't know you at all. You're a complete stranger and—"

"My point exactly." He folds his arms across his impressive chest and his T-shirt stretches across those beautifully sculpted pecs. His biceps bulge, drawing my attention to his thick veiny forearms.

My throat dries. My tongue seems to be stuck to the roof of my mouth. All the moisture in my body has drained to that single pulsing point between my legs. I gulp. "What…" I clear my throat, "What are you trying to say?"

"That you are too innocent."

I laugh, "Trust me, if you knew what I've been up to, you wouldn't say that."

His gaze narrows and color smears his cheeks. He opens his mouth, then closes it again. "What you have done or not done in the past is none of my business."

"Oh?"

He jerks his chin. "I am more concerned with the now, the present. The fact that you let me, a complete stranger, into your flat."

"You know what?" I scowl at him. "It's time you left."

"Oh, believe me, I am. I have no intention of staying, now that I know you are safe."

"The only threat here is from you."

"As I was saying…" he enunciates each word slowly, "you…allowed…me — someone you don't know — into your flat."

"You helped me earlier," I point out.

"I could have been simply trying to gain your trust."

"Is that what you were trying to do?"

"No." He blows out a breath. "I was trying to stop you from hurting yourself."

"So, you're not a stranger anymore."

"I was when you met me."

"Everyone's a stranger when you first meet them!" I throw up my hands. "You caught me at a weak moment, okay? And this back and forth is making my head spin. What's your point anyway?"

"That you shouldn't let anyone you don't know inside your home."

And sometimes, you shouldn't let even those you think do you know, because actually you don't…you don't know them at all. Damn you, Edward. I squeeze my eyes shut. "You are right. I'll be more careful next time."

"Good."

I open my eyelids to find him walking out of the kitchen. I reach for my hair band, find it's gone. Huh? I could swear I placed it on the table earlier. I shake my head, then rise to my feet and follow him. He snatches up the jacket he'd abandoned at some point on the arm of the couch; shrugs into it, then walks to the front door, opens it.

"Wait," I burst out. He pauses, turns to me. Waits as I try to figure out exactly what it is I want to tell him. What do I want from him? Why do I want anything from him? He's a stranger, right? So why doesn't he feel that way? Why do I feel like I already know him at some level? A wave of tiredness washes over me. I curl my fingers around the frame of the kitchen doorway where I am poised. "My name is Ava, Ava Erikson."

"I know."

"You do?"

He nods, then points to where I've placed my mail on the table near the doorway.

"Right."

He turns away, when I stop him again. "Wait." I call out to him and he stops, "Will I see you again?" I ask.

He hesitates then glances at me over his shoulder. "Do you want to see me again, Ava?"

2

Baron

She hesitates, glances away.

"Do you?" I persist. "Do you want us to meet again?" *What the hell am I doing here?* I'd been outside to ensure that she was fine. That she got back home safely. That she'd be okay…that I'd watch over her. That's what I had promised Edward when he'd called me earlier this morning.

It just so happened that it had coincided with one of my rare visits to London. I'd hauled ass from across town to ensure I was there before he left. Only I had missed him. By the time I'd arrived, asshole had taken off already. I'd tried calling him and had gotten the message that his phone was disconnected. Not surprising. It's what I'd have done if I wanted to disappear, and clearly, I have a lot of experience in that. What had packed a punch was the woman who had chased after him, only to trip and almost fall.

And I couldn't let that happen. Why had I promised to look out for her, when all these years I had wanted nothing to do with him?

Your guess is as good as mine.

Perhaps it's the fact that he picked up the phone and called me? Something I had simply not expected, not after all these years, not after how we'd fallen out. How we'd sworn never to have anything to do with each other. And yet, in his time of crisis, when he needs someone he can trust, he eschews the rest of the Seven and reaches out to me.

He could have done so at any time, considering he's the only one who's had my phone number all along, but he'd desisted. Of course, for Edward, it wouldn't have mattered if I had been in the same city. He would have never reached out to me.

And now he'd called me... So, it had to have been a life and death situation. I could have refused him, of course. Could have asked him to approach one of the others...but...I hadn't. Perhaps it's time for me to return and face the shit-show of life that I left behind? A life on the fringes of which I had stayed for the past few months. None of them—not even Edward—had known that, of course.

I'd returned to town to watch my best friends getting married, one after the other. From a distance, of course, I'd seen them find the happiness they deserve. I don't begrudge them that. They need every bit of brightness that their women bring to their lives. As Ava had, no doubt, brought to Edward's. Something he, clearly, hadn't been aware of.

And you know that's not true. The Edward I'd once known had been hell-bent on depriving himself of even the smallest pleasure life had afforded him. It's why he'd turned to the seminary. Oh, of course, he'd claimed he'd felt the calling, and while I don't dispute that... I am pretty sure that's not the only reason he'd decided to become a priest. It would have been the discipline, the extreme deprivation that the life demanded that would have attracted him to it.

And then when he'd found something...or someone, who had broken through that self-imposed exile of his, he'd decided to flee. Typical. And I understand why he did it. After all, I did it too.

I tilt my head, train my gaze on the woman who's responsible for bringing me back to my own life again. A woman with auburn hair, so similar to the one who occupies my mind. But Ava is not her. She can't be the girl I glimpsed twice in the past fourteen years. The first time I'd seen her. she'd been but a little girl and the second time, while she had been grown up, I had only glimpsed her from a distance. Yet there had been something about her that had affected me so much both times. No, Ava can't be her. It would be too much of a coincidence for that to happen. Also, she belongs to Edward, remember?

"Well, Ava?" I demand. "You haven't answered my question yet."

She blows out a breath, then draws herself up to her full height. "Yes," she snaps. "Yes, I want to see you again."

The breath I'd not been aware of holding hisses out of me. Christ, had I been that on edge? Why does it matter to me whether or not she sees me again? I'd returned only as a favor to Edward, to make sure that this woman—his woman—would be safe while he's off killing his devils or putting the demons in his head to rest, or whatever it is that ex-priests who are ex-friends do.

Typical Edward. When the going gets rough, he gets going. Much as I had done. When guilt had gotten too much to bear, I had raced out of there. I hadn't been able to put enough space between myself and the scene of my wrongdoing. And now, I am back…to face…my life. The remnants of it, that is. My friends, if they'll have me back.

And what I had been forced to do during the incident? That's gone. Over. In the past. Never to be spoken of again. Just as I'll make sure never to overstep the line with this woman. She is Edward's… All I am going to do is make sure that she stays safe… That I protect her from hurting herself, if necessary. Yep, I can do that. For Edward. For what I owe him. For the wedge I had driven between us, and which I have no intention of fixing, not for as long as I live. In fact, the reason I am back is because… Edward isn't here. It makes it so much simpler. Enough time to make amends, to make up for turning my back on my friends. I'll make the most of the time he is away to help his woman too. It's the least I can do for him.

"Good." I nod at her. "I'll be in touch." I shrug on my coat and walk to the door, then turn to level a glance at her over my shoulder. "Lock the door after me; don't open it for anyone you don't know."

She huffs, "Oh, please, I'll be fine."

"When it comes to your safety, I will not compromise. Do you understand?"

She blinks.

"Do you?"

"Y...yes."

"Good." I step outside, close the door after myself, and wait until the sound of the latch being snapped into place reaches me. Only then, do I turn and march down the steps. I stalk up the sidewalk to where I'd parked my SUV, get inside the car, then toy with the hair tie I had pilfered.

Why the hell did I do that? Why had I felt compelled to pick it up, like some teenaged boy in need of a memento from his beloved? Shit, it had been a moment of weakness, no doubt about it.

I stare at the purple-colored band, then bring it to my nose and sniff it. The scent of jasmine and luscious raspberries fills my senses. I am instantly hard. Hell! This instant response to her... It's disconcerting, to say the least. If I am not careful, I am going to become obsessed with her... Correction, I already am obsessed with here. It's why I am sitting here, outside her home, in my vehicle, thinking about her scent, the softness of her skin, those delectable, perfect curves of her body. How right she'd felt in my arms when I had carried her inside...

What in the bloody hell is wrong with me? I returned to do Edward a favor, remember? Best I not lose sight of that. I slide the hairband into my pocket, then ease onto the quiet street. By the time I reach my destination on the outskirts of the city, the sun is up in the sky.

I park my vehicle, peer through the windshield at the deserted warehouse. It's where I'd last seen the rest of the Seven. At the Kings of the Alley showdown when I'd taken on the guy fielded by the Bratva and not been able to defeat him. I'd had to pull out and Arpad had taken my place. And that's when Edward and I had fought—for the last time. And I had walked out. My fingers tighten around the wheel.

Of course, they would want to meet me here. The tossers aren't going to go easy on me. Not that I blame them. If it were me, I'd do the same. Bet they've spent long hours thinking up their revenge. Bet they'll take their time exacting it, too. It's the only reason I am hesitating to go in. Not because I want to delay the inevitable. Not because I've been dreading this reunion for as long as I've been gone. Only consolation, Edward isn't here. Which makes it both good and bad. If he were here, he'd deflect the attention from me, do his best to soothe out the tensions. Or maybe not. Perhaps he'd be the first to exact his vengeance. After all, I had wronged him… Almost as much as our kidnappers had. Shit! I slam my fist into the wheel, hit the button for the horn instead, which blares. The noise echoes through the empty parking lot, ricochets through my mind, careening me straight into an image from my past.

Noise, so much noise, loud noise that didn't stop. Day and night, and the next day again. On and on until I couldn't hear myself think or breathe or feel parts of my body that had seized up, grown numb. My lungs hurt, my heart pounded in my chest, and I couldn't hold back the saliva that drooled from my lips. They had found me wounded, separated from my battalion and had taken me prisoner. They had patched me up… But that was only so they could keep me alive long enough to question me. Which had been worse? Kidnapped at twelve during the incident and held for a month, or taken as POW at twenty-seven and being interrogated?

They had subjected me to the noise, the clanking, the thrash of heavy metal, the hard sounds that had reverberated through my skull, that stopped me from sleeping, from breathing… From living. *Oh, God, I want to die. Kill me, already. Now, right now.* I'd raised my eyes heavenward, and pleaded with whichever higher power was there watching over me. Please take me away, take me out of this pain, this misery. Put an end to this helplessness that grips me, this powerlessness that incapacitates me, this vulnerability that shrouds me, that wraps around my chest, my throat, that squeezes down so I can't breathe anymore. Can't breathe. *Breathe.*

In.

Out.

In.

I force myself to draw in the oxygen. Force my lungs to inflate. Deflate. Again. Focus on the small things. The smoothness of the steering wheel under my fingers. The scent of leather. The fabric of my T-shirt against my skin. The feel of my toes inside my boots. Breathe in again. Another breath. A third. Will my heartbeat to slow. My pulse rate to drop to normal. Then I straighten, open my eyes, wipe the sweat from my face. I turn toward the car door, only to have it wrenched open. I am hauled out of the SUV, and pushed to the ground. The impact of the crash reverberates through my body. I glance up to find my assailant standing over me. The sun slants in my eyes and I can't see his face. Then he bends to grab my collar again and a pair of familiar eyes fill my line of sight.

"You?"

3

Baron

"Get up," Saint growls.

I push myself up to a standing position. "I don't want to fight you."

"But I do." He lunges forward and his fist connects with my nose. Pain slices through my head. Sparks of red and white explode behind my eyes. I stumble back, straighten, sense him move and duck, out of instinct.

His fist whooshes by my face. The breeze from it lifts the hair from my forehead. He follows that up with another hit, this time to my side. Pain blooms up my spine. "Fuck."

He lunges forward, catches me in the stomach. The breath whooshes out of me. I double over, and he brings his fist up to connect with my chin. My head snaps back. Darkness overwhelms me.

Something wet licks my face, my nose, my mouth. I pry my eyes open to find a pair of doggy eyes staring down at me.

"Hey, Max, here boy," a voice calls... One I recognize as Sinclair's. The dog whines, glances from his master then back. He pushes his nose into my shoulder as if to apologize, then turns and darts off.

I groan, throw my arm over my face, and the movement sends a shudder of pain racing up my spine. Fucking hell. I draw in a breath and my throat burns. My ribs ache. My face feels like I've connected with a wall... Or Saint, in this case. Fucking Saint. I draw in a breath, and my ribs protest. My stomach lurches and I pant and stay still, hoping, praying, the sickness in my stomach will subside. I must have dozed off for a few seconds, maybe, when a touch to my shoulder has me jackknifing up to sitting position. Instantly, my head throbs, my chin hurts, and my stomach twists in on itself. I gasp, lower my head. Take in a breath and another.

"Easy now." A man's voice—another one I recognize—reaches me. "You're a little banged up."

"No shit." I tip up my chin and scowl at the familiar features of my friend. I clear my throat. "Hey, Doc. How's it going?"

He shrugs. "I guess we'll find out, once we work out the reasons behind why you left the way you did—"

"Not to mention, finding out why you're back," a low voice growls behind me.

I blow out a breath, turn to Saint, then wince when a throbbing slices through my head. "I know you're angry—"

"Angry?" he snaps. "You think I'm *angry*—?" His voice rises in tandem to the pain that thud-thud-thuds against my brain.

"From where I am, that's a calculated guess, I'd say." I raise my hand to shield my face from the sunlight that pours down on me through the windows high up in the ceiling. I move to the side, take in the features of my friends.

Saint stands with his hands bunched at his sides. Next to him, Damian's arms are folded across his chest. On his other side, Sinclair stands, his body relaxed. Next to him, Max whines and Sinclair bends to scratch behind his ear. He straightens, fixes me with an unblinking glare.

Weston walks around me to join the rest of the men. I recognize it for what it is. A show of unity. Four against one. Arpad's missing, probably because he's on his honeymoon. Yeah, I've kept tabs on my friends. I may have left London and my friends behind, but they never left me.

I push myself to standing and my side screams in protest. My face feels numb, my ribs twinge, and I bite down the groan that works its way up my throat.

"I take it you are not happy to see me?"

My voice echoes around the empty warehouse.

"Whose choice was it to meet here, anyway?" I glance at Sinner. "Can't be you, Sinner. You never did have a flair for the dramatic. As for you, Saint?" I train my gaze on him, "You're too hotheaded. When you're that angry, you can't think straight."

Saint growls, takes a step forward, but Damian stops him. "Easy there, he's baiting you."

"It could have been you, Damian." I twist my lips. "You were the dreamer amongst us. You aimed high—congratulations on the success of your last single, by the way. It hit me, bro; it broke me. It's the reason I decided to come back."

Damian stiffens, seems like he's about to say something, then stops himself.

"I heard the song and knew something had shifted amongst you guys. To see each of you find the loves of your lives… It made me believe again."

Weston shifts his weight from foot to foot. I turn my attention to him. "You did good, Doc. Not only did you qualify, you became a heart surgeon. Of all of us, you were always the most level-headed. You kept your eyes focused on the goal, the big picture. It's not easy to have achieved what you have… Not after what happened to us."

The silence intensifies. The men stiffen. I glance between them, then rub the back of my neck. "Yeah, took only ten minutes of us meeting for one of us to bring up the incident huh?" I say wryly. "Not that I haven't tried to forget it, but something like that… Well, the more I bury it, the more it's right in front of me, haunting me at every turn, you get me?"

The men meet my gaze. The expression on their features range from empathy to disbelief to anger.

"Look," I take a step forward, "I understand how it must seem from where you are, but trust me when I say that it was for the best. If I had stayed on, it would have only screwed things further. It was best that I took off the way I did."

Anger pulses from the group. Saint's knuckles are white tipped, Damian and Weston stiffen. The only person who seems unaffected is Sinner. Which only means that he is livid. Very livid. The anger pulsing behind that cool expression is probably far more lethal than the obvious rage evident on Saint's face. Shit. I have to find a way to defuse this situation, before one of us does something that we'll regret. And regret, we would. The five of them, including Arpad, may hate me now, but we need each other. Our strange, twisted relationship is the only thing that's real in the post-incident life that we lead.

"Edward," I swallow, "he took off this morning."

All four of them seem to freeze for a second, then Sinner jerks his chin. "We know."

"You do?" I turn to him, "How —"

"You didn't think we'd allow anything to happen to one of us without the rest of us being aware?"

"You had eyes on him?" I nod. "Good, then you were able to track where he went?"

"No."

"No?" I snap. "What do you mean no? We need to find him before he does something he'll regret. We need to make sure he's safe —"

"The only person he needs to be guarded from is you, and considering you are here and he isn't..." Sinner raises his shoulder.

"He wasn't in his right mind when he called me. He..." I rub the back of my neck. "He hurt the last man who walked into confession."

"That's when he called you," Sinner says slowly, "so you could take care of it?"

I nod. "When I reached the church, he was still breathing. I hauled him out of there, and took him to Weston." I nod in his direction.

"You could have mentioned something of what happened then," Weston mutters. "It's a good thing I'd never turn away any of you Seven, no matter how suspicious the circumstances."

"And I thank you for that." I tilt my head.

"Still doesn't answer who this man is, or why Edward lost his temper with him and almost killed him?" Sinner frowns at me. "At least, I am assuming that's what happened."

"Exactly." I rub the back of my neck. "From what Edward told me, the man walked in to confess. Edward decided to help him, even though it was after church hours."

"Typical Edward," Damian mutters, "always going out of his way to help others."

"Which makes it all the more intriguing as to what caused him to lose his shit," Weston murmurs.

"Only one reason he'd resort to violence," Sinclair states. He turns to take in the expressions on the faces of his friends. "You guys thinking what I am?"

"That it had to do with the incident?" Weston offers.

"It did," I confirm.

Sinclair's shoulders stiffen. A jolt of anger runs through the men. Sinclair turns to me, "We need to question the man."

"I will question the man—"

"What the fuck—!?" Saint explodes, and I hold up my hand.

"—when he regains consciousness. He's currently still out."

"Where have you kept him?" Sinclair's voice hardens. "Where are you hiding the motherfucker?" His gaze ping-pongs between Weston and me.

"I'm not hiding him. I simply took him to a safehouse where Weston is treating him."

All eyes turn to Weston who nods, "I am. Asshole's still unconscious but his condition is stable."

Sinclair turns to me, "And when he's awake I get to question him." He narrows his gaze, "I need to be there when the bastard opens his eyes."

"And you will." I widen my stance. "You'll be there watching with the rest of them, while I interrogate."

"Why you motherfucker—" Saint steps forward.

Sinclair places a hand on his shoulder. "Easy, Caldwell."

Saint makes a threatening voice low in his throat. "When I get my hands on you, I am going to—"

"Yeah," I blow out a breath, "still the same Saint. More anger than common sense. How you managed to find a woman crazy enough to put up with your shit, I'll never know. I—"

Saint lunges forward. Both Sinclair and Damian grab him and hold him back.

"Stop it, you two," Sinclair orders. He turns on me, "Apologize to him."

I glower at Saint. "Why should I?"

"Because what you said was unwarranted. We don't insult each other's families, or have you forgotten that in the time you were away?"

I wince. Then squeeze the bridge of my nose. "You're right," I mutter before turning my attention to Saint. "I'm sorry, that was out of line."

"What's out of line, is you deciding to drop back into our lives, and thinking that you can pick up where you left off," he snarls.

"That's not why I returned."

"No, you returned because Edward needed your help, though why he reached out to you, of all people, I don't understand."

"I had the necessary skills to take care of it." I draw myself up to my full height. "And maybe...he trusted me more?"

"Keep telling yourself that." Saint bunches his fingers at his sides, "Clearly, all those years you spent away haven't changed your capacity to delude yourself."

"Is that what you think?"

"Not just me," he retorts.

I glance around at the faces of my once friends, then stiffen. Their expressions are simply variants of the anger I see on Saint's.

"It wasn't just about the man," I finally say. "If it were, he could have just asked Weston."

Sinclair stiffens. "What other help could he have asked from you?"

I meet his gaze, fold my arms across my chest and wait. Wait.

Sinclair's forehead clears. "I see." He nods. "How interesting."

"What?" Saint whips his head around. "What the devil do you mean?"

Sinclair jerks his head toward me, "The Father didn't trust any of us enough for this, apparently."

"What bullshit," Damian bursts out. "Any one of us would have put our life on the line for Edward."

"Evidently, it's something he values more than his life. Who better than his once best friend to take care of that, hmm?"

"Values more than his life?" Saint glowers at me. "What could he have valued more — ?"

Sinclair unwinds his body long enough to clap his hand on the back Saint's head.

"Ow." Saint snaps his head around "What the fuck, Sin— ah!" He blinks. "You mean —"

Sinner nods. "Yes, dipshit. Exactly."

"Hmm." Saint turns and eyes me with a speculative gaze. "I see."

"What?" Weston glances between us. "The hell am I missing now?"

"Catch up, Doc," Saint drawls. "You're not normally this slow. Being married, plainly, has softened you too much around the edges."

"Speak for yourself," Weston says mildly. "I am guessing this is about a woman?" He tilts his head.

"Which woman?" Damian blinks, looks between us. "What the hell you guys talking about?"

"Ava," Sinclair clarifies. "Isla's friend, who was there at Arpad's wedding."

"She was?" His forehead wrinkles. "Guess I'll have to take your word for it. I might have been a little preoccupied with my new wife."

"You're forgiven, man." Saint smirks. "Pussy-whipped, as you are."

"And you aren't?" Damian chuckles.

I glance between them, realizing just how much I've missed this easy banter. It would be so easy to slip into that old routine with them. To be part of the Seven once more. Shit, I really have missed it, missed them...missed the camaraderie. Missed this sensation that there are people who care for me, who may hate me sometimes, but who care enough about me, to fight with me. People who have my back.

Saint holds up his hands, "Hey, I'll be the first to concede, having Victoria in my life has changed everything. Speaking of," he glances at his watch, "I need to get going, or I'll be late for the appointment with the midwife."

"Midwife." I stare at him. "You're going to see the midwife?"

"With Victoria, yes." He scowls at me. "It's known to happen."

"It is?" I stare at him.

"We're pregnant, you tosser."

"We..." I open and shut my mouth. "Did you say *we're* pregnant?"

"So?" Color smears his cheeks. He glowers back at me. "You have a point you're trying to make here?" He snaps, then straightens. "Why the fuck am I still talking to this guy, huh?" He glances around at Sinner. "What have we decided to do with him, anyway?"

"Do with me?" I scowl, "You guys aren't going to do anything with me."

"Oh, yes, we are." Sinclair cracks his neck. "You hurt one of us deeply when you left. Now, you're back and he's gone. And for some reason, he's asked you to keep an eye on his girl."

"Has he?" Damian frowns. "We only have this wanker's words to go on." He jerks his chin at me.

"I may be many things, but a liar is not one of them," I snap back.

"Hmm." Sinner strokes his chin. "I shouldn't, but I am inclined to believe you on that."

"You are...?"

He nods. "Sure, you're too smart to lie to us about something so important. Also, I believe that you are here to make amends to us; that you want us...and Edward especially, to forgive you."

I shift my stance. "And do you think you can?" I swallow. "Forgive me."

He looks me up and down. "No."

4

"Dancing lets me escape, it allows me to transfer my thoughts to the rhythm of the melody instead of concentrating on the depressing details of my teenage life..."
-From Ava's Diary

Ava

"Thanks, Ava, that was a great session." The last of my students waves at me as she departs the studio.

I gather up the scarves I'd used during the lesson, which had gone better than I'd expected, actually. Especially, considering that my mind had not been on it. How could it be, when it had been occupied with not one, but two men? How is it even possible that I've gone from being a virgin to being fucked thoroughly by a man who'd broken his vows for me…to being strongly attracted to another—all, in less than a week? Hell, in less than twenty-four hours!

Hell. I deposit the scarves in the basket at the far end of the room, then turn to where I'd plugged in my music. This had been my third class of the day and I still have too much pent-up energy in me. Maybe I should try to compose another routine? Something I could use in yet another Eastern-themed wedding that Isla has been asked to organize.

I switch on the music, and as the beats of *Kiss Kiss* by Tarkan fill the room, I close my eyes and sway. Shuffle my feet, shimmy, allow the rhythm to grip me, sway my hips, grind them, let the vibrations travel up my thighs, my belly.

"Holy shit, girl, you've got some moves."

I yelp, snap open my eyes. "Isla," I press my palm to my chest, "you scared me."

"Sorry." She holds up her hands. "I did ring, but you didn't hear me over the music, so I decided to come inside anyway. It's okay, isn't it, that I am here?" Her forehead furrows. "I'm not disturbing you or anything, am I? You did give me the passcode to the studio, after all."

"You're good." I turn and switch off the music.

In the silence that descends I feel my heart bumping against my ribcage. "It's all good." I turn to her. "I was just prepping for my performance at the next wedding you are organizing."

"Ah," she nods, "you mean Liam's wedding?"

"Liam's?" I gape. "You mean Weston's brother, Liam?"

Her lips turn down, then she smooths out her forehead. "The very same. He's marrying some society heiress or another. Which is great."

"It is?" I watch her closely.

"Of course, it is. The joining of two big families, the wedding of the year, almost as big as a royal wedding, and I get to organize it. It's going to be great publicity for my little company."

"So why don't you look happy?"

"What do you mean? Of course, I am happy." She pinches both sides of her lips, widens her fake smile until I am sure her cheeks hurt.

"Okay, that's creepy."

She switches off her smile. Lowers her chin. "You're right. I have mixed feelings about it."

"Because you like Liam?"

"Like?" She laughs. "That's not the word I'd use for how much I'd like to slap that annoying smirk off his face, right before I throw myself at him and lick those luscious lips."

"So," I say cautiously, "you do like him?"

"I hate him." She sets her jaw. "But we are not talking about him."

"We're not?"

"Nor am I here to talk about myself."

I peer into her eyes, then raise my hands. "Oh, no, no, no. I am not going to talk about it."

"Aww, come on, Ava. Let me, at least, live vicariously through you."

"What about the rest of the girls? Surely, being married to one of the Seven means they are having enough sex. They'll have much more to share with you."

"That's the problem. It's married sex, which is a bit like eating risotto."

I slow blink. "Let me get this straight. You're saying married sex is a bit like eating risotto?"

"Yep." She nods. "You know, it's rice and cheese and all the stuff that makes you warm and content and seduces you into a food coma, and you know you should stop eating, but you can't because all that serotonin has kicked in and made you happy, but really, it's weighing you down. But you don't realize it until it's too late."

I wince. "Unlike unmarried sex, which is like what? Chili-cake?"

"Precisely." She jerks her chin up and down. "Spicy and unpredictable and you never know when the taste is going to wallop you, and you peel back each layer and reveal a surprise... And then there's still the cream and—" She frowns. "Hold on, is there even a dish called a chili-cake?"

"Sure is." I nod. "It's a chili-laced chocolate sponge cake."

She wrinkles her nose, "Okay, not sure I'd want to eat that, but you know what I mean."

"Yeah." Though where I'm at now, it's more like being a patty in a hamburger, or the cream filing of an Oreo, if you know what I mean? I snort and Isla eyes me with curiosity.

"What's going on with you, Ava?"

"N…nothing." I walk toward the changing room adjoining the studio and she follows.

"It's something, babe, going by your expression."

I blow out a breath. Am I that transparent? But then, Isla has always been too perceptive for her own good. Besides, she's the only friend I am close enough to be able to confide in about what's happened, and I have to talk to someone about it. I can't possibly keep everything that happened bottled up inside. I push open the door to the changing room and walk in with Isla at my heels. I walk toward my locker, and pull out my street clothes. I need a shower, but I can take it when I get home. Instead, I strip off the yoga pants and my top and change into my leggings and a sweatshirt. Pulling on my shoes, then my jacket, I turn to her. "Edward," I murmur.

"What about him."

"He left."

"What do you mean, he left?" She frowns.

"He came to my place sometime early yesterday morning, then he broke his vows."

She stiffens, "He broke his vows. Is that a euphemism for—"

I nod. "Yeah. I chew the inside of my lip. We ah, did it."

"O-k-a-y." She lowers her chin. "Let me get this right. You and the Father had—"

"Sex." I blow out a breath. "Yeah. We did."

"Then he left?"

"He hopped on his bike and got out of there."

"How far could he get on a bicycle?" She laughs.

I roll my eyes. "A motorcycle, doofus."

"Ha-ha. Okay, but he's coming back, isn't he?"

"I…" I glance away, then back at her. "I'm not sure."

"Is there any reason you think he isn't returning? Did he tell you he wasn't coming back?"

"Yeah." I swallow.

"You sure about that."

"Let's see, his exact words were, 'I can give you something to remember me by.' And also, 'promise me you won't believe what you'll hear about me.'" I wipe away my tears. "And then, after he fucked me again the second time, he said that he had to go." I bite the inside of my cheek. "And PS, he also took my virginity."

"Virginity?" Isla stares at me. "Thought you said you weren't a virgin?"

"I lied." I brush away more tears. Shit, why the hell am I crying about him? A man who didn't hesitate to turn and leave, even after I begged him not to. He doesn't deserve me; he doesn't. "It still doesn't excuse what he did. He shagged me and then he left. I told him not to go. I begged him to stay. But he crept away from my bed while I was sleeping. The coward."

"Men," Isla huffs, "bloody wankers, the lot of them."

"They are." I nod "Especially Edward."

"Definitely Edward," she agrees. "He's a douchebag."

"The worst kind of douche there is. He's a motherfucking bastard and it doesn't mean anything that he broke his vows for me. Or that he did stay and hold me while I slept." I take in a shaky breath. "Or that he did come to me before he left. He could well not have. He could have simply crept away and then... I'd have never known that he had feelings for me. And that would have been better, right?"

"Oh, Sweetie." Isla looks at me with compassion, and that's the last straw. My heart shatters. The sobs well up and I bury my face in my hands and allow the tears to overwhelm me.

She reaches me, pulls me into an embrace and I wrap my arms around her. I bury my face in my friend's shoulder and allow myself to give in to the weeping. Just this once, I'll be weak. This once, I'll allow myself to pour out all of my disappointment, my frustration, my helplessness in not being able to see that I was setting myself up for heartbreak.

What the hell had I been thinking, allowing myself to be attracted to a priest? Worse, I'd fallen in love with him. It had happened so quickly that I hadn't been able to stop myself. Correction, I hadn't wanted to hold back. I'd seen Edward and something had shifted inside of me. That base part of me had honed in on him.

That primitive, feminine instinct in me had been attracted to him, hadn't cared that he had dedicated himself to God. Oh, how innocent I'd been. I'd seen him as a challenge, had wanted to woo him away from his chosen path.

I had succeeded. And now I have to pay the consequences for it. He'd come to me, with the intention of leaving. Hell, I never had a chance. He'd come to tell me goodbye, I realize that now. But as soon as he'd seen me, something had changed in him. He'd asked me if I wanted him to shag me and I… I had said yes. How could I have said otherwise? Why had he even asked the question? Why couldn't he have simply turned and left?

Would I have allowed him to do that?

Could I have let him walk out without…being with him? Why had I fallen asleep? Why had I not insisted that he fuck me again, and again, and again? So I'd have enough memories from one night to last me a lifetime. Shit, is that romantic? Or unrealistic? Or had I simply made the most of the opportunity I had been handed? If I had let him leave without sleeping with him, I'd have never forgiven myself. Truth.

And yet, he'd walked out on me. Had I slept with him hoping that it would change his mind? That once he'd been inside of me, he'd have never wanted to leave? A part of me had hoped… Okay, so I had staked my future on it. I had thrown myself into trying to please him, into being everything he wanted, and it had been incredible. The best experience of my life… One that I am not going to forget in a hurry—one I'm never going to get over. Let's face it, after Edward, after realizing what he'd given up to be with me, how he'd turned to me for comfort, how he'd fucked me everywhere, in every hole… How could I possibly find anyone else who'll compare?

Baron could. He's as intense, as gorgeous… There is something about him that resonates with me…in a different way. A darker way.

Where Edward was light… Baron is the other side. Like opposite sides of the same coin. Or the edge. That thing just out of reach that makes me want to grasp it. That hints at something hot and passionate just under the surface. I suppose they are similar in that way. Edward had been restricted by the bars he'd imposed on himself due to his calling. Baron…he seems to have simply locked himself away. He is unreachable, in a different way.

I step back, and Isla releases me.

She scans my features. "You okay, hun?"

"Yeah." I swallow, "What was the name of the seventh guy you mentioned, the one who disappeared after the incident?"

She searches my features, "You mean, Baron?"

I open and shut my mouth, "His name was Baron?"

She nods, "Yes... Why?"

Shit, no wonder his name had seemed familiar but I hadn't placed it earlier. Guess I had been a little preoccupied when I'd met him. Only with the man I'd thought meant something to me walking out on me. No biggie. Of course, I hadn't made the connection between my Baron—no, not my Baron—between the stranger whose name is Baron and the Baron who is one of the Seven. The Baron who is a mystery and a challenge… One… I have no intention of pursuing. No way, am I going to be interested in him. Not so soon after Edward. The last thing I need is a rebound affair…and especially, not this quickly after Edward, and not with someone who knows Edward. Not to mention, someone who didn't mention to me that he knows Edward. The blood drains from my face.

"Everything okay?" Isla asks

"No, but it will be." I rub my palm across my face, glance down at the splotches of moisture on her jacket. "Sorry, I spoiled your clothes."

"Oh, forget about that." She waves a hand in the air. "It will dry. Now why don't we get you home, and I can pour us both drinks and—"

A sound at the doorway, has us both turning toward it.

I take in the man whose shoulders fill the space, who's so tall that the top of his head seems to brush the doorframe.

"You?" I swallow. "How did you get in here?"

5

Baron

"I walked in." I growl.

"You need to be buzzed in at the studio door." She frowns. "You can't just walk in like that."

"And yet, I just did," I point out.

"What is that supposed to mean?" She blinks. "Did you just break in?"

"It took me exactly three and a half minutes to crack the code to your studio door," I growl. "And the front door to the building doesn't even have a lock."

She reddens.

"Your security here sucks, you know that?"

"You're exasperating, you know that?" she snipes back.

"You ain't seen nothin' yet."

"Oh, piss off," she mutters.

"I will, after I take you home."

"I can take the tube," she insists.

"It's not safe. I'll drive you instead."

"Says who?"

"Says me."

"And who are you to tell me what I can and can't do?"

"I told you, when it comes to your safety I will not compromise, Ava."

"I am safe." She scowls.

"Says the woman whose studio is in a building whose door doesn't even have a lock. Seriously Ava, you need to move your studio from this walking disaster zone of a place."

"Disaster zone?" She snarls, "You dare call the place I built with hard work and commitment, the first space I have created dedicated to my art, a disaster?" Her chest heaves and her cheeks redden.

Why do her eyes seem swollen? Was she crying again?

The woman next to her shifts restlessly. Shit, I had been so focused on Ava, I hadn't even noticed that there was someone else in the studio. So much for my security 'expertise.' And I had insulted her about something that clearly means so much to her, and that too, in front of someone else? Way to go, asshole.

I draw in a breath, then rub the back of my neck, "I apologize." I roll my shoulders, "I may have been out of line."

"May have been?" She arches a brow and I stiffen.

"I am sorry I insulted you about your studio." I glance around the space, "It's a beautiful space."

She narrows her gaze.

"Really," I turn to her, "I understand what it is to build something from pure passion."

"You do?"

I nod, "Of course. you'd have to be blind not to see how much this space means to you, Ava."

"Hmmph." She folds her arms about her waist. "Okay."

"So, you accept my apology?"

She seems like she's going to decline, then jerks her chin.

Thank fuck. "Doesn't mean the place is secure," I mutter and her gaze widens.

"We'll agree to disagree." She purses her lips. "What are you doing here anyway?"

"Came to see if you wanted a ride home."

When I'd left her after breakfast, she'd seemed like she was coming back to normal, but as I take in her features now, I notice the hollows under her cheekbones. Now that the flush on her cheeks from our earlier disagreement is fading away, she seems too pale. Her shoulders are hunched, and there's an overall defeated air about her.

Of course, it isn't that easy to bounce back from the kind of break-up she had. I should know. It took me years… No, I am still getting over it. So, how had I expected her to simply pick up the pieces and move on after Edward left, with no explanation?

Fucking Edward. I should have known he wouldn't be able to do justice to the one good thing that had happened to him. If she were mine, I'd…take care of her, protect her, make sure she never wants for anything. Make sure I do everything in my power to keep her happy. I can still do that. I can ensure that I distract her enough so she doesn't spend her time thinking about him.

I fold my arms across my chest, glance from her to the woman who steps in front of her.

"I'm Isla." She comes forward. "And you are—?" She holds out her hand and I take it.

"Baron."

"Baron," She nods, then her eyebrows shoot up. She glances up, peruses my features. "Not *the Baron*, Baron?"

I arch an eyebrow and she scowls. "I mean, are you Baron, one of the Seven? The Baron, who left all those years ago and only kept in touch on occasion, Baron?"

"And if I am?"

"Are you?" Her scowl deepens. "You are, right?"

I draw in a breath. "Yeah, I am, though if you ask any of the Seven, they'll say that I am not one of them anymore."

"Omigosh." Isla opens and closes her mouth. "You are back? Do the Seven know? Did you—?"

"Hold on." Ava steps up to stand next to her. "So now you are owning up to being one of the Seven?"

"Of course, I am." I glare at her, "Your point being—"

"You didn't mention it to me when you met me."

"You didn't ask." I raise my shoulders.

"You could have told me that you knew—"

"Edward?" I tilt my head, "I'm telling you now."

"So, you two have met?" Isla glances between us, "When did that happen?"

Ava flushes. "This morning, after Edward took off, I ran out of the house to follow him and fell. Baron, here, helped me. He, uh, took me inside."

"He took you inside?" She blinks.

"Yeah," Ava drags her fingers through her hair, "and made me breakfast."

"You?" She turns on me, "You stayed to cook for her?"

I hold up my hands. "I was simply making sure that she was okay, before I left."

"Hmph." She purses her lips together. "That's all you did?"

"Honest." I turn my gaze back to Ava. "I was simply worried about her. And if you don't mind, I want to speak with her."

Isla folds her arms across her chest.

"Alone."

Ava tips up her chin and holds my gaze.

"Please?" I add. "Can I speak to you, Ava?"

Ava swallows, then nods, "Okay."

"You don't have to do anything you don't want to, Ava," Isla warns her. "If this guy is bothering you—"

"He's not," she replies.

"You sure?" Isla turns and grips her shoulder. "I can ask him to leave, if he is."

Ava meets her gaze, the two seem to have a silent conversation, then Isla blows out a breath. "Fine, I'll go then."

She turns back to me. "I have my eyes on you." She glowers. "If you hurt her in any way, you'll have me to contend with, and I warn you, it won't be good for you."

I lower my chin. "I promise, I won't harm her or cause her any kind of pain." *Not unless she asks.*

"Hmm." She purses her lips, "We'll see." She turns to Ava, kissing her on her cheek. "You take care, doll, and call me if you need anything."

Then, she brushes past me and leaves.

Ava glances at me, before moving to the side of the room. She grabs her handbag and hooks it over her shoulder. "I was just leaving."

She tries to brush past me, and I plant my body in her path.

She sighs, "Really? You are going to do this now?"

"Why were you crying?"

"I wasn't crying." Her lower lip trembles.

"Yes, you were."

"No, I wasn't." Her chin wobbles; her features contort.

"Shit, shit, shit." I haul her to me and she buries her head in the stretch of shirt between the lapels of my jacket.

I wrap my arms around her, hold her close as she sobs. My chest hurts, the blood pounds at my temples, and anger slices through my head.

Damn you, Edward, for breaking her heart.

And then, you had to hand her over to me, knowing I'd be attracted to her. Knowing that I'd want to protect her. You knew what it would do to me to find her so helpless, didn't you? You knew I'd give anything to be there for her in any way that she needs. You knew I'd be loyal to you. That I wouldn't betray you. That I'd be attracted to her and yet hold back, because she belongs to you. How dare you put me in this situation, you asshole? How could you ask me to look out for her, knowing every second of every minute that I spend with her, I'll want to make her mine? Fuck you, Edward! I hope you find no peace, wherever you are. I hope you spend each second missing her, knowing that I am here for her when you should be here taking care of her.

I tuck her head under my chin, rub soothing circles across her back. When she only cries harder, I scoop her up, walk over to the chair in the corner and lower my bulk into it. The chair creaks, but holds. I rock her in my arms, hum the first tune that comes into my head.

I'm not sure how long this goes on, but slowly, her sobs subside. She hiccups, draws in a breath. Her shoulders tremble, and I pull her even closer. She pushes her nose into my shirt, and inhales. And again. I pause, glance down at her, "Did you just sniff me?"

She pauses, then nods.

"Does it help?"

She nods again.

"Okay then."

I continue to hold her, until she pulls away. I loosen my arms about her, and she leans back, tips up her chin and glances at me from under her eyelashes. "Didn't mean to fall apart like that," she mutters.

"You are entitled."

"No, I am not. I've had enough of being the victim here. I hate crying, you know. Always have. It took me a full two weeks to break down after my mother died."

"I'm sorry." I peer down into her features. "Truly."

"Thank you." She nods. "She was unwell. Cancer." She swallows, looking down again. "She was ailing for nearly a year before she died…and it was a relief when she was gone, because she didn't have to suffer anymore. Does that make me a terrible daughter? That I was happy that she was finally out of pain?"

"No," I grip her hand between mine, "no, it doesn't."

"I didn't want to lose her, but I couldn't stand to see her suffering. And then…after she died, I found out that she had asked my father to marry her best friend after she was gone." She swallows. "That's the kind of woman she was. Always looking out for everyone else. Everyone except herself. She was too focused on her daughters, her husband. She didn't take enough care of herself. It's why she fell sick, I'm sure of it."

I run my fingers through her hair, tuck a strand behind her ear.

She tips up her chin, holding my gaze. "You knew Edward?"

I stiffen, then force my shoulders to relax. I knew this conversation was coming. Only, I'd hoped to have a little while longer before having to reveal how I'd happened to be there at the very moment that she'd run after Edward, but no matter. There is never going to be a good time for it, I know that. Still, it doesn't help when I glance into those big green eyes of hers and see the hurt in them. I wince, glance away, then back at her.

"I did," I clear my throat, "I do know him."

"So, you know that..." She swallows. "You know that he and I—, that we—"

"Fucked?"

She hunches her shoulders, pushes away from me. I release her and she slides off my lap. Her bag slides to the floor, as she begins to pace in front of me.

"We slept together... once... no, a few times that night, before he—"

"Stop." I bunch my fingers at my side, "I don't need to know the details."

"Why not?" She turns and stares at me. "Don't you want to know what he did to me the first time we were together? How he..." She swallows, "how he, took my arse."

I bunch my shoulders.

"How he came in my mouth."

My thigh muscles spasm, my stomach ties itself in knots.

"How he took my virginity when he—"

I spring up, walk over to her, slap my hand across her mouth. "Enough, woman," I roar.

My voice echoes around the space.

She blinks up at me, big green eyes that carry the remnants of grief from her mother's death, from Edward's desertion, from how she misses him. Shit, despite what he did to her, she still misses him.

I lower my hand to my side. "I made a mistake. I shouldn't have come here."

"No, you did the right thing," she says in a hard voice. "If you hadn't, I wouldn't have realized that Edward's friend is as unfeeling as he was."

"I have no idea why you're jumping to that conclusion."

"Oh?" She chuckles. "You just show up out of nowhere and don't tell me you know Edward?"

"I know it seems odd that I was there at the very moment that Edward left—"

"Odd?" she snarls. "Of course, not. Why should it be odd that as Edward leaves my life, his friend enters it? Then pretends he is concerned about me."

"I was—am concerned about you."

"Then appears to take care of me—"

"I did take care of you." I set my jaw, "I want to take care of you."

"Why?" she says in a low voice. "Why the hell would you want to do that?"

"Because Edward asked me to."

6

Ava

"Excuse me?" I shake my head. "What the hell did you say?"

"I said," he draws himself up to his full height, "that Edward asked me to watch over you."

"Hold on." I hold up a hand, and take a breath. "He asked you to look out for me?"

He nods.

"Edward knew he was leaving, so he called you and asked you to be there when I fell apart? He knew I'd fall apart. Of course, he did." I drag my fingers through my hair, then begin to pace again. "He knew I was weak. Knew I was in love with him, that I was falling for him and—"

"You were in love with him?"

"Yes, of course, I was." I pause, stare at him over my shoulder. "Why else would I collapse in such theatrical fashion when he decided to take off?"

"You didn't know him that long…"

"How do you know that?" I frown.

"When Edward called me, he gave me the highlights of, uh, how you guys met."

"He did, did he?" I fold my arms around my waist. "Geez, like this isn't weird at all. The man I fall for, not only is he a priest, but before he breaks his vows and takes off, he calls up his best friend—"

"Not his best friend"

"—to come by and take care of the woman he fucked—"

"You're more than that to him."

"—before he decides to take off without a word of explanation."

"He had a good reason."

"Oh, so now you're defending him?" I slap my palms on my hips. "Of course, you are. You men stick together, regardless of the fact that he and you—" I stab my finger at him, "are in the wrong."

"I am not defending him, and he is in the wrong."

"As are you."

"What did I do?" He stares at me. "I was trying to help you."

"You were trying to help me?"

"You know I was."

"How? By forgetting to mention to me that you knew Edward? By acting all solicitous when you were probably laughing at how broken down I am?"

"I didn't laugh at you, and you know that."

"Why would you agree to what Edward asked of you anyway? Why would any man agree to keep an eye on the woman his friend shagged? Unless—" I lower my hands to my sides, "Oh, I see."

"What?" He scowls. "What does that mean?"

"I understand now why you are doing this."

"Do you?" His expression grows wary.

"Of course, I do." I allow a smile to curve my lips. "You probably figured; you'd get me to trust you. You'd worm your way into my affections, so I'd spread my legs for you."

"Stop that," he growls.

"Why? Isn't that the truth?" I grip my breasts and squeeze. "Don't tell me you didn't think of it."

"I..." He wets his lips. His gaze drops down to where I am massaging my breasts. His chest rises and falls.

"Don't tell me that you didn't see me and think that you wanted some of it. That it didn't cross your mind to fuck me as well."

"I... I." His throat moves as he swallows. Then he firms his lips.

"What? Not so cocky now, huh? Why are you silent? Why can't you tell me what you were thinking of all along?" I shrug out of my jacket, let it drop to the floor. Then slide my hand down my stomach to the apex of my thighs. "Bet you saw me and wanted to get inside my pants. Bet you saw me and thought I would be an easy conquest, that you could shag me anytime you wanted and I wouldn't deny you."

He closes the distance between us, places a finger across my lips. "Shh," he murmurs, "don't do this."

"Why not?" I lean away and he drops his hand to his side. "It's true, isn't it?" I ask. "Tell me you didn't think of screwing me when you saw me."

"I did."

I blink. Heat courses through my veins. My core trembles. Even as something hot stabs at my ribcage. I fist my fingers at my sides, tip my chin up. "Well then, there's nothing more to say, is there?"

I bend to pick up my jacket, but he's already there. He straightens, holding it out for me. "That still doesn't negate the fact that I was there to take care of you. To ensure that you didn't do something you would regret later."

"What, like kill myself?" I mutter.

When he doesn't reply, I stare up into his features. "Shit," I swear. "That's what he was afraid of? He was worried that I'd be so heartbroken that I'd put an end to my life? Why, the ego of that man." I draw myself up to my full height. "As you can see, I am fine and coping well enough without him. Or you, for that matter. You've done your job, so you can leave now."

He simply jerks his chin toward the jacket.

I glance at it, then back up at him. "What are you still doing here? I told you, you can go."

He doesn't react. His stance indicates he'd be happy to simply stay there until I do as he asks.

I blow out a breath, turn and slide my arms through the sleeves of the jacket. He smooths it over my shoulders, and the heat of his big palms radiates through the material and into my skin. A shiver slides up my spine. He steps back, picks up my bag and hands it to me. Then he walks to the door and holds it open for me. I walk over to him, reach for the light switch, but once more, he beats me to it.

He switches off the light in the dressing room and I step through and into the studio. I walk through to the main exit. He follows me, flicking off the lights before he reaches me. I scowl at him. He simply arches an eyebrow. He holds the door open again and I step through into the corridor. I walk out, lock the door behind me, when the light in the corridor flickers and goes out.

"Damn it," I grumble, "I should have gotten that fixed."

I take a step forward and connect with something hard and solid. The scent of crisp mountain air and pine trees envelops me. Then he wraps his hand around my shoulder. "Stay here," he rumbles.

"Not going anywhere, considering I can't see—"

A light flickers through the darkness. I blink, glance up to find him towering over me. I know he's big, I've seen him in broad daylight, but in the darkness, he seems larger than life. Big. Vital. Strong enough to weather any storm. Solid enough to lean on. I could pour all of my worries, my troubles, onto his shoulders and he would take it.

The air between us shifts, thickens into something hot and lusty and... My thighs clench. I lower my gaze and look away. He clears his throat, turns to shine the beam ahead, lighting a path through the darkness. "Come on." He grips my hand and his warm, thick fingers encircle my wrist, making me feel small and fragile in comparison. My nerve endings pop. Heat twists my lower belly. I bite down on my lower lip, allowing him to lead me across the corridor, down the flight of stairs, and out through the front door and onto the sidewalk.

Once there, he releases my hand, and of course, I miss his warmth. Shit, this is not right. How can I be so attracted to him, so quickly, when just a few days ago I'd been obsessed with

Edward and couldn't stop thinking about him? Clearly, I am on my way to becoming a slut. Someone with no loyalty, someone who lusts after every good-looking man who happens to cross my path.

And that isn't true either.

I don't lust after everyone. Only Edward…and now him. Baron. One of the Seven. Edward's friend. Someone who hadn't revealed to me the real reason he'd been there to help me when he first met me. Do all the men in my life have to turn out to be such douches?

I pause. Baron takes a few steps forward before he turns to search for me. He frowns, angles his body toward me. I shake my head. "We're done," I mutter. "I don't want to see you again."

"Now, hold on—" He takes a step forward and I throw up my hand.

"I don't know what game you and Edward are playing, but I want no part of it."

"No games, Ava, honest—"

"You think I am going to believe you after what you revealed earlier?"

He scowls. "I expect you to think this through rationally."

"Oh, but I am. After what Edward did to me, the last thing I am going to do is have my emotions involved in any decision. It's why I am saying with complete confidence that I don't want anything to do with you."

"You don't mean it."

"I've never meant anything more in my entire life."

He takes a step forward and I hold up my hand. "One more step, and I swear, I'll scream."

His shoulders bunch. He glances around the deserted road then back at me. "At least, let me see you back home."

"No, thank you."

"It's not safe for you to head back on your own this late," he insists.

"It's nine p.m."

"It's late."

"I can take care of myself." I draw myself up to my full height, which still means I only come up to the level of his chest. "I've been doing so all these years."

"That was before."

"Before what?"

He hesitates, "Before I came on the scene."

"Nothing's changed, then, for it makes no difference to me. You're still not in my life, in any form. This association, whatever it is between us, ends here."

"No," he grinds out.

"Yes." I tip up my chin. "You don't get a say in it. I don't want anything to do with you, Baron."

Turning, I walk toward the tube station. The hair on the back of my neck prickles and I'm sure he's following me. I will not look back. Will not give him the satisfaction of finding out that he makes me nervous. By the time I reach the tube station I am out of breath. I duck inside, walk through the ticket barriers, and onto the platform. Only then, do I allow myself to glance down the platform. I don't see anyone who looks like him. Whew. Okay. That's good, right? Doesn't mean that I am disappointed that he took me at my word and gave up the pursuit so quickly.

I get into the tube, find a seat and collapse. In twenty minutes, I am walking up the street, heading to my place. The itch at the back of my neck appears again. This time, I glance over my shoulder, but don't see anything. Strange. Is he here? Did he found a way to conceal himself so I don't spot him? I increase my pace, reach home and lock the door behind me. Only then, do I heave out a sigh of relief.

I head for the bathroom, have a quick shower, then dress in my pajamas. I pour myself a glass of wine. Slouching back against the sofa with a bowl of noodles—yeah, instant, I know, not good, but damn, if all that MSG doesn't taste delicious just now. There is something about cheap cup-o-noodles that takes me right back to my uni days when things were simpler. Also, because I'd preferred to do then exactly as I am doing now—slurp down noodles, swig down wine, and watch my favorite show on TV…. Which, by the way, hasn't changed either, for I flip on the TV and tune into *Twilight*.

On screen, Edward watches Bella as she's sleeping. Yeah, so it's stalkerish, but for some reason, that scene always gets me.

Maybe because the thought of being the focus of someone's attention in that singular fashion is mind-boggling. And erotic, and such a turn on. Gah! Oh, Edward. Why the hell does he have to share the name with my favorite fictional character?

I turn off the TV, walk to the kitchen and wash my bowl in the sink. After rinsing my wine glass, I turn off the light and head for my bedroom. Yawning, I walk to the window and peer out. That's when I notice the SUV parked outside on the road. I can just about make out the shape of the person behind the wheel. It can't be. Surely not. I peer through the glass, try to discern the features of the man… And it is a man, that much I can tell from the shape of the shoulders, the way his head is turned…in my direction. And in my imagination, the intensity of his perusal heats my blood.

Shit, it can't be him. Is it? It must be. My instinct tells me it has to be him, that there is no danger from whoever is in the car. What the hell is he doing here? Is he watching over me?

The way Edward watched over Bella? But this is not Ed. This is Baron, remember? Shit, I am tying myself in knots. I step back and the drape falls into place. Moving over to the bed, I slide in between the covers and switch off my lamp. I turn over, snuggle into my pillow and my eyelids flutter down.

When I wake up, the light slants in through the open window. Whoa, guess I managed to sleep through the night. I jump out of bed, pad over to the window, lift the drape to find the SUV still in the same position as last night. I peer through the window, make out the shape of the man behind the wheel. His figure is slumped back. Is he asleep?

I turn away, walk out to the kitchen, make some coffee, then set about making breakfast. I sit down to avocado on toast, lift the mug of coffee to my mouth, then grimace. Shit, I am going to do this, aren't I?

I get up, pour some of the coffee in a travel mug, then fashion the extra toast and avocado I made into a sandwich, adding cheese and tomatoes to it. Yeah, it's vegetarian, but too bad; that's all he's getting in this house.

Piling the food into a takeaway container, I place it in a brown paper bag, and carry it with me, along with the mug. At the door, I step into my boots, grab my keys and step out of the house. I head down the path, cross the road, and walk around to the driver's side of the car. Before I can tap on the window, he rolls it down. Of course, he is awake and alert. He had to be to keep watch. Somehow, I just know that he hasn't slept a wink during the night. Adamant man.

I hand over the paper bag and the takeaway mug. He nods his thanks, takes a sip of the coffee from the mug, then sighs his gratitude. He places the mug in the cup holder, opens the container and digs in. I watch with some satisfaction as he finishes every last bite, then proceeds to drink the coffee. When he's done, he places the container inside the paper bag and hands everything over to me.

"Thanks," he nods, "but you didn't have to."

"I'd have done it for anyone," I mutter, "so don't go getting any ideas."

He tilts his head, surveys me closely. "What ideas would that be?"

"You know. That I've forgiven you for what you did."

"That's not why I'm doing this." He jerks his chin toward the dash.

"Yeah," I blow out a breath, "I need to get back."

I step away, aware that he's watching me as I head back inside the house. Shit, me and my soft heart. I should have simply let him be, not bothered to give him food. But seriously, how could I go about my breakfast, knowing he had spent the night outside in his car and not do something for him? Argh!

I get dressed, leave the house and walk past the SUV to the tube station. When I emerge on the other side, I don't look around for his car. Even if I had I wouldn't have spotted him. He's too good at this...whatever he does. What is his profession, anyway? Had he been a cop at some point, that he hadn't thought twice about shifting into surveillance mode with me? Well, whatever.

I walk up the steps and into my studio. For the next two hours, I devote myself to perfecting my new routine before my afternoon class. The day goes by quickly and after my third and final class, I go about shutting down for the night. I emerge into the crisp night air, spot the SUV parked across the road again.

Of course, he's been there all this time, keeping watch over me. It feels weird...strange... Good? Yeah, it feels weirdly reassuring to know that he has my back. Not that I need protection, despite what he said. I am an average girl living in London. There is no reason to think I am in any kind of danger.

Still... It is comforting to know I have my own guardian angel watching over me. Shit, I have to stop thinking of him in those terms. His presence is getting to me, that's all it is. I pause, wondering if I should go over and tell him not to tail me anymore... As if that would stop him. If anything, I'd be playing into his hands if I did that. No, I am going to have to simply ignore him. That is the only way out.

I head back to the tube station and then home.

This routine continues for the next four days. How the hell he manages to keep up the surveillance on his own, I don't know. The only time he seems to sleep is in the car at night. Yet when I take him coffee and breakfast in the mornings, he doesn't seem to be run down. Most times, we don't speak either, except for the occasional and very civil good morning to each other.

Ha, he doesn't fool me, though. That civility is just a front for the barely civilized intensity he's hiding inside. And every time I see him, it's like he's a blow to the chest. How can I feel so connected to someone I've just met? How can it be happening all over again? Each day, I manage to tear myself away from him. Then, I get dressed, go to work, return, all with the SUV trailing me to and from the tube station on either side.

The nights... Despite the fact that my dreams are filled with Edward, it's Baron's face that I wake up with first thing in the morning. Shit, this isn't good. Not at all. Things are getting so muddled up in my head right now.

On the fifth day, I wrap up my last class, and step outside, then glance across the street to find the SUV missing. Huh? I glance up and down the street, find no car, no man. Well, that didn't take long, did it? Guess I wore him down.

I trudge to the tube station. Why had I thought that he'd hang in for longer, that he'd continue to follow me day in and day out...for how long? To be honest, I'd hoped for a few weeks, at least, if not a month. And he'd lasted, what, four days? And he said Edward had asked him to take care of me. Whatever. I snort, pull out my phone and call Isla.

"Hey babe, where have you been?"

"Just work, been busy you know?"

"Anything to do with Baron?"

"Baron?" I frown. "Why do you ask?"

"Only because he showed up here, and now, he and Sinclair are locked in some kind of argument."

Here? "Argument?"

"I hear the sound of something crashing in the background."

"Strike that." Isla's voice rises in excitement. "Sinclair just socked Baron in the jaw."

"What?" I tighten my grasp on the phone. "What do you mean, he hit Baron? Where are you?"

"At Summer and Sinclair's townhouse." More noises, the sound of something hitting the ground, something big and heavy and—

"Shit, are they fighting?" I scowl.

"More like walloping each other," she mutters. "Whoa, this is something. Nothing like two alpha males going at each other to get the blood flowing."

More sounds of yelling reach me over the phone. My heart begins to race and my blood thuds at my temples. "What the hell is happening there?"

"Ooh." I hear Isla pulling in air between her teeth. "That was a bad hit. Baron's down."

"Wait, what?" I stiffen. "I'm coming over."

7

Baron

"Fuck you, asshole!" Sterling glowers down at me.

Bitch had gotten in a good hit; he'd managed to get through my defenses…because I'd let him. Don't tell him that. I'd been parked outside Ava's studio, waiting for her to finish, and following up on my various business interests via phone and email when Weston had called. Of the remaining Seven, he's the only one who's reached out since the last fight. He'd said he couldn't break rank with the rest, that they were all livid with me for what they'd seen as my desertion, but that if I wanted a chance to talk to them, now was my chance. The five of them and their wives had gathered at Sinclair's home, and if I wanted an opportunity to plead my case with them, I'd best get my arse over there. I had hesitated, hadn't wanted to drive off and leave her unescorted, especially not now that night had fallen. But I couldn't miss this opportunity. I had to get back into the circle of trust… This is the only family I know… Also, I need them on board for what's next.

So, I had reached out to someone I know I can trust. I'd asked Archer—my friend and business partner with whom I had started the security business after leaving the army—to step in for me. Archer had served with me in the army. Hell, it was because of him that I had joined the army in the first place. I trust him to watch over Ava.

As soon as he had arrived, I'd taken off to Sinclair's town house.

Weston had been on hand to let me in. He'd led me into the living room where the rest of the four, including Arpad, who had returned from his honeymoon, had been gathered around the bar.

Sinclair had taken one look at me, and after scowling at Weston, he'd asked me to step out.

We'd each taken off our jackets and shirts, then circled each other, as the rest had come out to watch.

Each of us had waited for the other to make a move. I'd waited, waited…until he'd launched himself at me. Then we had gone a few rounds. I'd given as good as I'd gotten, then realized this was one fight I had to lose…for the greater win. If this is the only way to get Sterling to speak to me, so be it. So, I had allowed him to get the punch in.

Now I glower up at him, not needing to fake the pain that slices through my head. Bastard had managed to bury his fist in my forehead. Good thing I have a hard head. Still, the cut across my eyebrow is bleeding down my face. I use my arm to wipe away the blood, then hold out my hand to him.

He hesitates, reaches for me, then seems to change his mind at the last minute. He straightens, turns and walks off toward the house.

I stare after him. Anger pulses through me. "Don't turn your back on me, you motherfucker."

He pauses, turns to glare at me over his shoulder. "You may have fucked yours, but I never did."

Rage fills my head. My vision tunnels. I stagger to my feet, then rush him.

He turns back, lowers his head and charges. We meet in the middle. Or rather, his head connects with my middle. The breath rushes out of me. Pain coils out from where he head-butted me. I stagger back as he punches me in the side, and the other, follows with an upper cut. He raises his fist again and I catch the hit on my arm. Throw up my other arm to deflect the next, then rear back and manage to land one in his solar plexus.

I am going to lose; doesn't mean I have to roll over and play dead. If I did that, asshole would suspect me anyway. No, I am going to push back now. I swing again, plant one on his shoulder, then his side, then the other. He punches up, catches me under the chin. I stumble back, and he raises his fist. This time, there is no pretending. I know he's going to knock me down and I am ready. I glare at him, head on, wait for his fist to land, then he straightens.

He stands there panting, his chest rising and falling in tandem with mine. Sweat drips down his torso and mine. My chin thrums, my shoulder protests. Blood drips from my cut, onto my chest.

He straightens, his glare intensifies, then without a word, he pivots and walks off.

Saint glares at me, before he turns and follows.

Damian jerks his chin at me.

Arpad walks up to me, holds up his fist. "Good fight."

I frown.

"Go on, man," he urges, and I fist bump him. "Like old times, huh?" he mutters. "Good to have you back, Baron."

A hot sensation stabs at my chest. He turns, stalks off as Weston approaches me. "Let's get you cleaned up."

Ten minutes later, I wince as Weston stitches me up in one of the spare bedrooms that he's taken over as his temporary surgery.

"Shit, I need a drink."

"You do know it's all a myth…right?"

"What?" I scowl, then grimace when a pulse of pain radiates out from the cut. "If you're talking about me, then I am legend, of course, when it comes to fights."

"I don't know, man. The last time I saw you fighting the Bratva, you lost."

In more ways than he'll ever know. I fold my fingers into fists. "I definitely need a drink."

"Having alcohol doesn't really help numb the pain," Weston mutters. "It's a myth propagated by Hollywood that the whole world has bought into."

"What-bloody-ever," I mutter, "I could do with some whiskey right now."

"Here." Arpad ambles in with a bottle and three glasses. He tops up the glasses, hands one over to me, then sets one aside for Doc, before turning a chair to straddle it.

"So, you came back, eh?" He raises his glass at me.

I glower at him, then throw back my liquor. The alcohol burns its way down. It hits my stomach and heat radiates out from the impact.

"And you got married." I hold out my glass; he tops me up again. This time I hold up my glass, "Congratulations, man."

"Yeah." He grins and his entire face lights up.

"Whoa." I stare at him. "I take it, you're happy?"

"Delirious." He laughs. Asshole fucking laughs.

"Shit," I mutter. "You really do love her."

"I do." He chuckles. "It shows, eh?"

"Like a neon light," Weston says from next to me.

"Is that a subtle barb, Doc?" Arpad smirks. "Because I recall a time, not too long ago, when you walked around wearing a grin that stretched from ear to ear, right after you wedded a certain pastry chef."

"No, I didn't," he mutters.

"You did." Arpad laughs.

"I was merely on top of the world after snatching up the feistiest, sassiest, sexiest woman alive."

"Hey," Arpad scowls, "that was supposed to be my dialogue."

Weston leans back. "There. All done."

I touch my forehead and pin-pricks of pain radiate out from the touch. Nothing I can't handle.

"Once the endorphins wear off, the pain's gonna kick in some more."

I nod.

He writes out a prescription, hands it over. "Take the antibiotics to prevent infection. Keep the wound dry."

I stare at him.

"You know the drill, of course." His gaze narrows.

I tilt my head. "I don't know what you mean."

"Hmph." He scowls. "Wherever you've been, whatever you've been up to is not my concern...Actually, strike that." He shrugs. "It is my concern, as a friend. But as a doctor, it's clear to me that this isn't the first time you've been hurt, so, you don't get to hide from me, pal."

I merely arch an eyebrow, wince when my hurt forehead protests.

He blows out a breath. "Have it your way, but your scars don't lie." He points to the evidence on my shoulders and my back. "They tell me everything that you won't," he adds.

I bark out a laugh. "I leave six boys who don't know their heads from their arses and come back to six men who have their heads up their arses."

"Poetic." Arpad nods. "What have you been up to these last few years, anyway?"

"Hold on," Damian stalks in, "I want to listen to this as well."

"It's not fucking story time," I growl.

"Oh, I don't know, I could do with a bedtime story." Weston tops me off, then Arpad, before handing the bottle to Damian.

He fills up his glass. "Should we toast?"

"No," I snap.

"Yes," Arpad counters.

"Definitely." Damian raises his glass. "To old friends."

"To new memories," Weston drawls.

"You mean new mammaries, don't you?" I mutter.

He stares at me. "Only one set of mammaries for me, ol' sport." He winks. "And don't talk about my wife that way."

I blink. Shit, things really have changed and I've missed it all. Missed my friends growing into men, missed how they'd met their women, missed how they'd become more grounded, more serious, more stable. There is a contentedness to them that… I don't miss at all. No, of course, not.

"Right." I raise my glass in his direction. "I apologize."

"Accepted." He swigs back his drink. "Speaking of, I need to —"

The door is pushed open and Ava tumbles in. Hair flowing to her waist, flushed cheeks, bright eyes, her gaze finds mine, unerringly, connects and holds.

The breath rushes out of me. I stare back, rake my gaze from the purple tips of her hair, to the bag she has clutched to her side, to the pointed, purple tips of her boots, then back to her face. "What are you doing here?"

8

Ava

He glares at me. I take in his broad shoulders, the acres of cut muscle, the corrugated abs, the concave stomach, the jeans that cling to his powerful thighs. He shifts his position and I jerk my chin up, and spot the new stitches on his forehead. I draw in a breath. "You're hurt?" I take a step toward him and he freezes.

"Are you okay?"

"Don't I look okay?" he growls.

"Uh, you look a bit beat up, to be honest."

"A bit?" Weston snorts and Baron sets his jaw.

"Why did you come?" He scowls.

"Hello to you too," I quip as I walk inside the room. Four sets of eyes follow me. "Isla told me you were hurt, so…" I toss my hair over my shoulder. What the hell am I doing here, anyway? I'd heard her say that Baron was down and something inside of me had pushed me to his side. I'd grabbed a cab—a freaking expensive ride which had cost me nearly forty pounds—gah! And made it here in record time, and the arse that he is, he's glowering at me like he's displeased about seeing me.

"Well, as you can see, I am fine," Baron snaps.

"And in your usual growly-pants mood," I mutter.

"Growly-pants?" He growls—no surprise there—then frowns. "What does that mean?"

"She means you're being a bitch." Weston rises to his feet. "And in all honesty, I agree."

"You stay out of this," I say at the same time as Baron.

Weston looks between us. A speculative look comes into his eyes. My cheeks heat. I know what he's thinking. He's seen me with Ed, and now, here I am checking up on Baron. Hell, the questions I see on his face. I have the same ones for myself. Only, I don't have the answers either.

Weston opens his mouth as if to say something, then shuts it.

"What?" Baron snaps. "Why don't you spit it out already?"

Weston scowls at Baron. "I hope you guys know what you are doing," he mutters.

"Why don't you stay out of this?" Baron glowers.

Weston bares his teeth. "Surely, you know that being part of the Seven means we are always up in each other's business?"

"Don't remind me." Baron rubs the back of the neck. "And you guys blame me for staying away for all these years?"

"You're back though, Baron," Weston's frown deepens, "which means, you need to play by the rules."

"As if any of you guys did?" Baron mutters. Weston opens his mouth and Baron raises his hand. "Stuff it," he barks. "Honestly, Wes, back the fuck up already."

"See?" I stab my finger at Baron, "See what I mean? Growly-pants. Definitely growly-pants."

He whips his head around and his gaze narrows. A vein throbs at his temple. "I don't need you here, either," he snaps.

"Too bad, I am here already." I move further into the room and the other men rise to their feet as one.

"Uh, I think Amelie's calling me." Weston places his glass down on the table with a thump.

"Yeah, me too. I mean, not Amelie, but Julia." Damian turns to me. "Hey, Ava. How's it going?"

"I'm good." I smile brightly at him and another growl rumbles from the asshole still sitting.

"I didn't see Julia on the way in," I say.

"Oh, she's not here." Damian smiles. "She's, uh, been a little under the weather."

"Is she okay?" I purse my lips. "Maybe it's the flu; everyone's been getting it."

Damian flushes. I blink. Uh, strange... Didn't think these men could look uncomfortable if they tried. Apparently, I was wrong.

"Yeah, she's good." Damian coughs. "All good."

"You won't be if you stare at her for much longer," Baron mutters.

"Whoa." I turn my head to scowl at him. "That wasn't very nice. You should apologize."

"Yeah," Damian smirks, "apologize, asshole."

Baron's jaw hardens. I frown at him, and he blows out a breath. "I apologize," he finally says.

"See, that wasn't so bad." I blink my eyelids at him. He lowers his chin, and his lips twist. My stomach jumps in response. Shit, that's hot. That mean look he has going there... It's potent and sexy and dangerous. My panties dampen. I twist my fingers into the material of my bag, hold his gaze.

Weston swoops up the soiled cotton, and the bandages. He thrusts them into a plastic bag. Then pulls off his gloves and deposits those too. He rises to his feet, grabs that bag in one hand, his doctor's bag with the other. "Right-o. I'll see you folks later." He walks toward the door, closing one eye as he passes me.

Damian nods at Baron, smiles at me. Baron frowns and Damian gives him the bird before sauntering out.

"Guess I'd better get going too." Arpad glances between us, then places his glass down on the table. He comes toward me, grabs my shoulders and kisses me on both cheeks.

Baron makes that growling noise again, deep in his throat. Arpad chuckles. "You take care, Ava."

He steps back, touches a finger to his forehead. "See you, Lieutenant."

I whip my head around in his direction. "Lieutenant?" I frown. "Did you serve in the army?"

Baron stares at Arpad. "How did you know?" he finally asks.

"You didn't think we'd have let you go without finding a way of keeping tabs on you." Arpad half smiles. "We lost your trail after you were discharged."

"Discharged?" I glance between them. "When were you discharged?"

"Two years ago," Baron mutters. "I was wounded in battle, then captured by the enemy."

"Wounded? Captured?" I feel the blood drain from my face. "How long were you — ?"

"Six months." He murmurs.

The blood drains from my face, "You were a POW for six months?"

His features harden.

Behind me, Arpad walks to the exit. "I'll let you two catch up." I hear him leave, and the door closes behind him.

In the silence that descends, I am suddenly aware that we are alone. I glance around the room, at the view outside the window, then down at my feet. Anywhere, but at the man glowering at me from the chair.

I shuffle over to the chair Arpad just vacated… It happens to be the chair farthest from Baron. I sink into it, place my bag on the floor, then link my fingers together. Why had I come? Why did I feel compelled to get here? I should have gone home… Nah, I'd have never been able to do that. Not after how he's become a constant in my life. In just one week, he's become a stabilizing influence. Like Edward had been? Same, but different. Ed had been a strike to the heart…but Baron… He is chipping away at the barriers I've built around myself since I was a child.

I'd been overweight and way too conscious about it. I'd always felt like I stood out. It's why I'd retreated into myself, found solace in music and books. It's why dancing is so important to me —a way to embrace myself, my imperfections, to be free of judgment. When I dance, there is no me… There is only the rhythm and the ability to get lost in it. To forget about the world and all of my worries, to transcend to a space and time where there is only the now.

The hair on the back of my neck prickles. I glance up to find his gaze trained on me. Those cold blue eyes seem to have lightened in color until they resemble chips of ice. A frost that could creep into my blood, cut through the bone and change me forever.

I shiver.

"Are you cold?" He frowns.

"N…no."

I peer at him from under my eyelashes, take in the hard planes of his face, the square jaw, that thick upper lip, the puffy lower lip that I want to dig my teeth into…. What the hell? Why is it that every time I set eyes on him, my intentions always go there?

I glance away. "I shouldn't have come."

"No, you shouldn't have."

I stiffen.

"But I am glad you did."

I jerk my head toward him again. "You are?"

He surveys me a little longer, then nods. "Sure, this makes my job easier."

I snap my shoulders back, rise to my feet, "If you are going to insult me —"

He blows out a breath, raises a hand. "Sorry, that was out of line."

I stay where I am, watch him as he seems to struggle with some emotion. Then, he points to a corner of the room. "Hand me that shirt, will you?"

I walk toward the bed, where someone has flung down his shirt. Pick it up, and the scent of him is suddenly there. Dark, edgy, masculine, laced with that scent of crisp mountain breeze and pine trees that I've come to associate with him. I walk over, holding it out. He reaches for it and our fingers touch. Goosebumps sizzle up my skin. I retract my hand, and glance up to find that he's watching me carefully. Did he feel it too? He must have. A pulse tics at the corner of his jaw. He shoves one arm into his shirt, reaches for the other and winces. Sweat beads his forehead. "Fuck," he growls under his breath.

"Let me," I offer before I can think otherwise. Stepping into the space between his legs, I lower the shirt on his shoulder to give it enough slack, then reach for the other sleeve. I hold it down so he can wrestle his arm into it, then slide it over his shoulder.

The tips of my breasts graze his chest, and his body goes solid. His shoulder muscles tense. A cloud of heat seems to spool off of him and slam into my chest. I swallow. My nipples harden until they throb. My toes curl. Moisture pools between my thighs.

"Ava," he whispers.

"Y…yeah."

"You're stepping on my foot."

"Oh." I gulp. "OH."

I glance down to find that, sure enough, my one booted foot is squarely on his much bigger, broader, wider, also-booted-but-in-Doc Martens foot.

I step off of him, backing away.

The oxygen rushes into my lungs and I gulp it down. My head spins. It's only because I'd forgotten to breathe there for a few seconds. That man… Holy hell… Standing close to him was like being faced with a furnace… Or being at the edge of a tornado. Or both. Throw in some thunderstorms, and hail... Well, add in all the fury of nature and you'll understand what I mean. It was like being on the edge of an incline, glancing down at the slope that led to a crazy jump, and knowing that once you set down the course there was no turning back. I stumble back, hit my chair and sit down again.

"I… I guess… I should leave." I clear my throat.

"You should."

I sneak a peek at him, take in the shirt that he's not yet buttoned. The column of his throat, the smooth expanse of ripped abs, the smattering of hair between his pecs. My stomach trembles and my thighs clench. I grip the arms of my chair.

"But you won't," he rumbles.

"What?" I frown at him. "What do you mean?"

"You know what I mean."

"N…no." I fix my gaze on him. "No, I don't."

"You do." His lips curl. Oh, Hell, why does his smirk have to be that hot? That sexy. That mean…with a dollop of cruelty.

Argh. Stop it. Stop eating him up with your eyes, bitch. And just over a week ago, you'd been salivating over a hot priest. The one who ran out and left you on your knees…literally. Ugh. I've had enough of the Seven. I should get out of here. I should. I push my heels into the floor, rising up to my feet.

He follows my every move; the skin around his eyes creases. He watches as I take a step forward, angle my body. I should turn. I should go. I swallow, put one foot in front of the other. I reach him, pause in front of him. His gaze heats. He tips his chin up, leans back in his chair, then he widens the space between his thighs.

Don't look down, don't. I lower my gaze, take in the thick bulge outlined at his crotch. Instantly, my core clenches. Moisture pools between my legs.

I swallow, rake my gaze up his chest, to his face, to where his blue eyes peruse me with frank curiosity. He's waiting to see what I'll do next. Hell, *I'm* waiting to see what I'll do next.

I shift my weight from foot to foot, twist my fingers together in front of me. *What do you want? What do you want to do? Do you want to stay? Do you want to go? Fuck it. I should leave.* I turn away. That's when he grabs my wrist.

9

Baron

What the hell are you doing? Let her go. Unhand her, you bastard. She's not yours. She's his. She belongs to a man you've have avoided for more than half your life. So why the hell had he called me and asked me to take care of her while he's away? Knowing Edward, it's because he's testing me. But why is he doing that? Why go to this extent to put me in temptation's way?

Why test me in the first place, when he knows the first chance I get, I'll betray him?

I tug, and she stumbles back. Her hair flows about my face and I inhale. The scent of jasmine and raspberries, warm, sweet, and lush. Like her curves. Like the flesh between her legs, which would be wet and throbbing and willing. If I reached around and cupped her pussy, would she arch back and into me? Would she part her legs and allow me full access to her slit — to the cradle of civilization that exists between her full thighs?

A trembling seizes her. Her hips twitch and her waist shimmies.

The dancer in her emerges, takes over, as if she senses that she is in danger.

I tug again and she turns toward me, her tiny waist at the level of my eyes. I release her hand, only to plant my palms on her hips. She shudders. Her breathing speeds up. I lower my chin, bury my nose in her crotch. A moan bleeds from her lips.

I draw in a deep breath and the scent of her ripens, the sweet scent of her arousal filling my lungs. The blood rushes to my groin and my dick throbs against the constraints of my jeans. I nuzzle into the apex of her leggings. She groans. I tighten my hold on her, tilt my chin up and flatten my face against her pussy. A whine trembles up her throat.

"Baron," she whispers, "please."

The sound of my name from her lips, her pleading tone... All of it rushes to my head. I close my mouth around her core and she hisses. I fasten my teeth around the fabric of her leggings, and through it, on the swollen nub of her clit. She cries out, digs her fingers into my hair as I begin to fuck her pussy with my mouth, through the barrier of her leggings. She parts her legs, gives me more access, and I slide my hands down to cup her generous hips. "F-u-c-k." I squeeze her flesh and she shivers.

I tilt her hips, opening her up further as I continue to suck on her, eat her out through the bloody cloth that covers the singularly most delicious, most erotic part of her. Her entire body jolts. She tugs on my hair and my scalp tingles. Tendrils of pleasure flash down my spine. My cock thickens even more and I thrust my tongue into her fabric outlined slit. She cries out again, digs her fingers deeper into my hair, thrusts her hips forward and into my face. I bite down on her pussy once more and her body trembles. Through the fabric of her leggings, I scent her arousal deepen. I glance up at her and command, "Come." And she shatters. Her eyes roll back in her head, she cries out, then slumps against me. I cup one palm against her butt, bring the other down between her thighs. I grind my heel into her clit, massage her pussy as she trembles and shudders in the aftermath of the orgasm.

"Oh, my god," she mumbles. "Oh, god."

"God has nothing to do with it." I lean back as she opens her heavy eyelids and stares down at me.

She opens and shuts her mouth, then shakes her head as if to clear it. "Did I...did I come?"

I set my lips, "It would seem that way." I set her away from me, then rise to my feet.

"I'll bring you home."

"Wait, what?" She blinks, sways a little and I grip her shoulder until she seems steadier on her feet. Then I step back. I smooth down her sweatshirt, so it covers her luscious hips, and hides the apex of her thighs.

"What are you doing?" She scowls down at herself.

"Making sure you are covered."

"Covered?" She stares a second longer, then color flushes her cheeks. She glances up at my face. "Oh."

I button up my shirt, then move around and past her. "Coming?"

"I already did."

A chuckle barks out from me. I turn and level a gaze at her. "Sassy, huh?"

She tips up her chin. "You have no idea." She marches up to me, then plants her hands on her hips. "What was that about?"

"What was what about?"

"That," she stabs her thumb over her shoulder, "whatever that was."

"I was simply proving a point."

"And what would that be?"

"That I can make you come"

"So can I," she tosses her hair back from her face, "make you come, I mean."

"Not interested."

"Is that right?" She closes the distance between us, then plants her palm on my swollen crotch. "That's not what this feels like."

"It's a normal reaction to what happened; doesn't mean I am going to follow through with it."

"Why not?" She squeezes down and my pulse rate speeds up.

"Don't do it," I growl.

"Worried you won't be able to hold out?"

"The only thing you need to be worried about is saving yourself," I warn.

"What the hell does that mean?" She massages my cock and the blood empties to my groin.

"It means," I grip her hand and push it into my crotch, "you don't want to do this."

"I do."

"No, you don't."

"Why not?" She scowls, then slides her hand down to cup my balls. "You want this, so why won't you let it happen?"

"Because I made a promise."

She swallows. "To Edward?"

"And to myself."

"And what promise is that?"

"That I'll never hurt you; that I will take care of you while he is gone."

"What if I want you to hurt me?" She steps closer and my throat dries. My balls tighten; the band around my chest constricts until I can't breathe.

"What if this is how I want you to take care of me?" she whispers.

Her green eyes dilate until there's only a circle of green around the pupils. I drag in a breath, and fuck me, but I can smell the sweet scent of her arousal. Ripe and luscious and ready for the picking. My throat dries. I squeeze her hand, then pull it away and to the side.

"You'll have to find someone else to scratch that itch." I make sure to curl my lips. "I am not going to settle for Edward's seconds." I say this despite my indisputable hunger to dive in for a second helping.

Her gaze narrows. Color flushes her cheeks. She pulls her hand from my hold and brings it up, but I am already moving. I grab her wrist, wrench her hand behind her. The action bows her spine, thrusts out her breasts until they are flattened against my chest. The shape of her curves, those hard nipples that dig into my front. *Fuck me.* My thighs go hard and my dick thickens. I tighten my hold, pull her closer…closer…dip my chin until my mouth is poised over hers. Until we are sharing breath.

Until I can see the freckles that dot her cheeks, and fuck me, if I don't want to lick her right there.

She flicks out her tongue to wet her lips and my gaze darts to her mouth. Fuck me, but I want to kiss her. I need to taste her. Just once. I want to swipe my tongue across that honeyed mouth and swallow her up completely. The blood pounds at my temple and my heart hammers in my chest. I lower my mouth to hers.

10

Ava

His gaze narrows and his chest rises up and then down.

I swallow, bring down my eyelids, then part my lips, waiting… waiting. He releases me so fast that I stumble back. He brushes past me, heads for the door and stalks out. *Shit, shit, shit.* What the hell was that? Why the hell had I come onto him so strongly? It's like when I am with him, I lose track of who I am.

How had I acted so wanton? How could I have thrown myself at him, so quickly after Edward? This… Whatever it is between us, is doing my head in.

I march down the steps, head to where I'd deposited my coat and bag in the living room of the town house.

As soon as I walk in, Isla rushes up to me. "Are you okay?" she whispers.

"Yeah… No." I shake my head. "I don't know."

I shrug into my coat and grab my bag, then glance past her to where Summer is watching me with sympathetic eyes.

"Want to talk about it?" she asks.

"Maybe later?" I half smile.

"Hang in there." She jerks her chin toward the hallway. "So, you and Baron?" She wrinkles her forehead. "Everything okay there?"

Ha, if she only knew.

"It's fine." I flash her a smile. "I'd better go; he's going to give me a ride home." I turn past her and head for the hallway when she calls out.

"Hang in there, Ava, it'll get better."

I laugh, "Nothing can make this better."

"Don't give up too quickly."

I pause and stare at her over my shoulder.

"What are you trying to say?"

She comes toward me, "That things are never what they seem with the Seven."

"That's putting it mildly." I bite the inside of my cheeks. "It's just… I feel…"

"Confused? Conflicted?" Isla pipes up.

"All of it, and more." I squeeze my eyes shut. "Everything is happening so fast, and I can't keep up."

"Maybe you are resisting too much?" she replies.

I open my eyes, scowl at her, then turn to Summer, "Do you feel that way, too? Do you think that I am fighting the inevitable?"

"If it feels this difficult, maybe."

"But…but…" I grip my bag at my side. "Surely, it can't be right that…"

"That you are attracted to Baron?"

I flush.

"I thought I was attracted to Edward."

"Who's not here anymore." Isla taps her chin "But Baron is."

"Doesn't mean I have to give in to the chemistry between us."

"So, there is chemistry between you two?" Isla asks.

"You don't know the half of it. It's like when we are in the same room… It's—"

"Madam." A plummy voice interrupts. "Mr. Baron's asked me to convey to Miss Ava that he doesn't like to be kept waiting."

"Of course, he doesn't." I turn and huff at the butler who stands by the doorway to the hall. "You can tell him to—"

"Yes Ma'am?" he says politely. Bet if I told him to tell Baron to go sod himself, he'd convey the message in that polite, affable tone too. I blow out a breath, "Doesn't matter."

I turn to the girls. "I gotta go."

"This conversation is not over," Isla warns.

"Yeah, yeah." I turn to leave and Summer calls after me, "Join us here on Friday night? Just us girls."

I raise my hand as I follow the butler out of the house. He walks me down the steps, holds the door open for me.

"Thank you." I smile at him as I clamber inside the SUV.

He shuts the door, and I stare ahead as Baron pulls out onto the road. We don't speak for the duration of the ride. When we reach my place, I push open the door and am out of there as soon as he parks. Gah, that was the most uncomfortable twenty minutes of my life, ever. I flounce across the sidewalk, up the garden path, reach the front door and am about to open it, then stop. I glance over my shoulder to find the SUV still parked there. Is he going to spend the night in the car again? Of course, he is. Damn him, and after everything that happened earlier... The best thing to do would be to let him spend the night in the car. Again.

I bow my head. *Don't do it. Don't do it. Damn it.* I turn and march back to the car, then around to the driver's side. He lowers his window as I reach it, then arches an eyebrow at me.

"You may as well come inside the house."

He glares back.

"I mean, come on. It's stupid that you spend your nights here in the car, when there's a perfectly good couch in my living room."

His forehead wrinkles. "I don't think that's a good idea."

"Sod that." I scoff. "I can keep my hands off you, if you can do the same."

He scowls.

"And after your earlier demonstration, clearly you can restrain yourself."

His jaw tics. His nostrils flare and he seems to be on the verge of saying something, then seems to change his mind. He rolls up his window, pushes open the door. I step back, walk over to the house, and unlocking the door, step inside. Placing my bag on the table in the hallway, I shrug off my coat. Then, grabbing my bag, I head to my bedroom. I deposit my bag on the side table, grab a pillow and a cover from the closet, then walk into the living room. Ignoring his bulk looming by the window, I deposit the bedclothes on the couch.

"There's only one bathroom," I nod toward the bedroom, "if you want to use it, while I get some water to drink?"

Without waiting for his reply, I walk toward the kitchen, drink some water, then grab a couple more bottles of water. By the time I reach the living room, he's seated on the couch. He's removed his shoes and socks, and as I place the bottle of water on the coffee table, I notice his bare feet. Large feet. Blunt cut toenails. I swallow. Suddenly my chest feels too tight. Heat flushes my skin. Moisture laces my core. I straighten, "Goodnight," I mutter, as I head for my room.

"Goodnight, Ava." His low rumble courses down my spine, igniting pin-pricks of lust in its wake. Oh, Hell. This is bad. A very, very bad idea. I shut the door, then hesitate. Should I lock it? If I did, he'd hear me lock it. Not that I don't trust him to not come in here. Question is, do I trust myself not to go to him at night? Gah! Get a grip. Think of Edward. Ed. The man you've been masturbating to until a week ago. The asshole priest who broke his vows for you. Then left you. I draw in a breath, shrug out of my clothes, and toss them over a chair. Then, pulling on a camisole, I slide into bed. I can't stop the yawn that cracks my jaws. I shut off the lamp and am asleep as soon as my head hits the pillow.

His scent reaches me first. Cut grass and mint. I watch as his powerful shoulders cut through the water. He swims across the length of the swimming pool, reaches the side and hauls himself up. The water sluices from his shoulders...as he swings his legs over the side. His thigh muscles ripple, his concave stomach tenses, and he straightens. He walks toward me, his huge shoulders blocking out the light of the sun, the rest of the scene behind him. His chest planes flex and the tendons of his beautiful throat move as he reaches his hand out to me. I rise to my feet, move to him, arm outstretched. Our fingers connect. Heat vibrates up my arm and my stomach muscles clench. He pulls me to him and my chest connects with his wet torso. A giggle bursts from my throat and an answering smile curves from his lips. His amber eyes gleam, then he dips his head, closes his beautiful lips over mine. Moisture pools in my core. My heart begins to race. He thrusts his tongue inside my mouth, swipes his tongue across my teeth. My belly trembles. He scoops me up in his arms, walks over to a deck chair and lowers me onto it. He follows, covers my body with his, and the weight of him presses me down. My nipples tighten and my thighs spasm. He peers into my eyes, that golden gaze of his lit from within. He cups my cheek, touches his forehead to mine. "I need you," he whispers. "I want you. I can't live without you. You're what grounds me to this life. Without you, I am no one."

I frown up at him, reach to smooth out the wrinkles on his forehead. "Edward I—"

"Shh." He lowers his head, brushes his lips over mine. "Don't speak," he whispers. "Just feel." He pushes his hips into mine and that hard length of his stabs into my core. "See what you do to me, Eve?"

"Ed," I swallow, "why did you leave?"

"It's the hardest thing I have ever done. I couldn't be with you, Eve. I wasn't good for you, in the state I was. But I didn't want you to be alone."

"You didn't?"

"No." He kisses my eyelids, the tip of my nose, my mouth. "I couldn't be there for you, so I did the next best thing. I asked Baron to take care of you."

"Baron?" I frown. "What do you mean, Ed."

"You'll know when you feel it."

"I hate riddles," I pout.

"And I love you."

My eyelids snap open. I stare into the darkness. What was that? What a weird dream. Why had I dreamed that? I turn over on my side, throw my leg over my pillow. My core clenches. The remnants of the dream cling to my skin; the scent of him still envelops me. The strength of him, as if imprinted into my muscle memory. The way he'd covered my body with his, how that thick length of his had pushed into my core. I slide my fingers down to cup my pussy through my panties. Shit! The fabric is soaked. I dig the heel of my hand into the fabric and massage my clit. Pinpricks of pleasure shoot out from the contact. My breasts seem to swell, and a groan wells from my lips. What am I doing? What is wrong with me? I thrust my hips against my hand, wanting so much to shove my fingers inside my own pussy. But it wouldn't be enough. I need something bigger, thicker...wider...ugh! No choice. I reach for the drawer on my bedstand, when a groan reaches me.

I freeze. Wait, arm outstretched. Am I dreaming? No, I am awake... What was that? I focus on the darkness. Wait... Only silence reaches me. I lower my hand and my fingertips brush the handle of the drawer when another groan filters through from the direction of the doorway. No, I definitely hadn't imagined it. I swing my legs over the side of the bed and straighten. Another groan, this one more strident, more urgent. I rush to the door, open it and step out into the living room.

Moonlight filters in through the crack between the drapes. I can make out the figure on the couch as he moves, thrashes around. I head toward Baron, stand over him as his features contort. Sweat gleams on his forehead, across his shoulders—his bare shoulders. Shit, of course he'd taken off his shirt before falling asleep. The cover gleams against the burnished brown of his torso. The fabric dips around his waist as he flings his arm over his forehead and groans. Moisture glistens on his cheek. Wait. Is he crying? Are those tears? Can't be. But why not? Can't grown men cry in their sleep?

His shoulders bunch and the tendons of his throat move as he swallows. Then his fingers bunch on the sheet, his knuckles white as he grips the fabric. Another low groan rumbles from him and my heart stutters. I lean forward and touch his shoulder. His eyes fly open. The next second, the world tilts. I am on my back on the floor and Baron's fingers are around my neck.

11

———————

Baron

"I am going to kill you," I growl. "I am going to tear you from limb to limb for what you did to me. Get your hands off of me, you filthy bastard." I squeeze down with my fingers, intent only on cutting off his air supply. If I could only snuff out his life, everything would be so much better. If I could only—

"Baron," her voice chokes. "Please…please…"

All thought empties from my head. I glance down at her delicate features, the auburn hair about her shoulders, her gaze wide, the green pupils dilated with—fear. Her pink rosebud-mouth open, as she chokes, and tries to draw breath.

"No." I release her and she coughs, draws in a breath, then another. She brings her fingers to her neck, presses her palms to the skin there. Her chest heaves as she coughs again.

"Fuck," I growl. "Fucking fuck." I scramble away from her, hit the side of the settee. "Fuck, I am so sorry, Ava. Fuck, fuck, fuck." I bury my fingers in my hair and tug. "I am so fucking sorry. What the hell is wrong with me?" I lower my hands and stare at my palms. "I almost killed you. You are not safe around me. This is why I should have slept in the car. I shouldn't be allowed anywhere near you. What the hell had I been thinking, allowing myself near you—?"

"Baron!" Her voice reaches me.

I ignore it. "I should have shot myself a long time ago. I am not fit to survive. I shouldn't have accepted Edward's call, shouldn't have come here in the first place."

"Baron, stop." She sits up, and crawls over to me. "It wasn't your fault. You were sleeping. You didn't know."

"That's not an excuse." I stare at my palms, the lines that run across the width. "I could have killed you, Ava."

"You wouldn't have."

"You don't know that."

"Of course, I do. Protecting is in your DNA; it's woven into every cell of your body. Someone like you, who would give your life for another, would never kill."

"That's where you are wrong." I glance up at her. "I have killed more people than you can imagine."

"That was war, you didn't have a choice."

"You always have a choice." I fold my fingers together. "I just chose to ignore it."

"You did what was right," she insists. "You did what you were told."

"You know what the worst part of it is?"

She shakes her head.

"I enjoyed it. I enjoyed killing."

She pales.

"I was so good at it, they pulled me off the frontlines."

"They did?"

I nod. "Turns out, there's one thing I am better at than killing, and that's torturing the enemy for their secrets."

"Torturing?" She swallows. "You tortured people?"

I peer into her features. "That was my specialty, you know?"

"What do you mean?" She frowns.

"That was my job, in the army. To torture enemy soldiers for information. I was so good at it that they gave me a fucking medal for it." I laugh. "They didn't know that the only time the voices in my head fell silent was when I was sussing out their weaknesses and using them against them."

She sits back on her haunches. "You were still doing your job."

I laugh. "You don't understand." I lower my hands to my side, "I fucking stood over grown men, used their fears and their life stories against them. I knew exactly how to take their worst terrors and deploy them to find weaknesses in their psyches. I knew how to break them down and rebuild them again."

"You...you brainwashed them?"

My lips twist. "I made them into weapons who could be redeployed undercover. I made them believe in their new identities enough for them to be sent back to their own countries. I sent them to their inevitable deaths."

"And in doing so, you helped many more lives back home."

I frown. "You think you know everything, don't you? You think you can view me with the same fucking rose-colored lenses as you viewed Edward?"

Her lips thin. "I didn't have to view him through anything. He was...good, inside and out."

"Oh?" I look her up and down. "And what about you, Ava? Was it good for you with him?"

"I am not answering that." She folds her arms across her chest. "You're hurting, I understand that. Doesn't mean you need to insult Edward or what...we had."

"And what did you have?" I sneer. "A few fucks before he left? The man was so afraid of what he felt for you, he couldn't even stay to face the consequences of his actions."

"He...he needed time to sort things out."

"He's so weak, he couldn't even stick to his chosen path. He walked away from the very profession that he claimed meant everything to him."

"He did it for me," she snarls. "Everything he did, he did it for me."

"He did it for himself." I allow my grin to widen. "You were just an excuse. Just easy pussy that he couldn't resist, he —"

She swoops out her hand and I grab her wrist.

"Don't even think about it," I warn.

"And what will you do, huh?" She holds my gaze. "You going to torture me like you did those prisoners? You going to pull your gun on me? Or better still," she reaches for my other hand and brings it to her neck, "you going to finish what you started? You going to choke me, Baron?"

I place my fingers in the exact same marks where my fingers had rested a few minutes ago. "Do you want me to…?" I wind my fingers around her neck. "Do you want me to choke you, Ava? Is that what this is about?"

"No." She swallows and the action sends vibrations shuddering across my palm. My dick twitches. Fuck, what the hell is wrong with me? Why does her fear, her wide-eyed gaze, the way her breathing speeds up —why does all of it only arouse me more?

"You're lying." I lower my voice to a hush, "You want me to hurt you, don't you? You want me to show you how it could be to walk that thin path between pleasure and pain."

"No." She shakes her head.

"You want me to tip you over the edge so you can forget him, so you can discover parts of you which you don't even know exist."

Her chest rises and falls. "You're wrong." She licks her lips; her gaze darts to the side then back at me.

I rise up on my knees, and loom over her. "You want me to fuck you."

"No," she tips up her chin, "that's not true."

"You're right."

She frowns. "I am?"

I lower my head until our eyelashes tangle. "You want me to not just fuck you, you want me to demolish you and build you back again as I did those prisoners."

Her lips part. The breath whooshes out of her, "No, I don't."

"You do."

I rake my gaze across her features. "Even now, you're imagining how it would be if I were to push you down on your front and mount you from behind. How it would feel to have my cock deep inside your most forbidden places. How you want me to remove every single imprint he left on your body and replace it with mine. How you want to be commanded, to be subjugated, to be told what to do every moment we are together. You want me to take your choices and give you a space where you don't need to think. Where you don't need to worry about the world outside. Where it's just you and me and our shared filthy passion. Where you could ask me to do every single depraved thing you ever dreamed of and things you didn't even know were possible. Where you'd spend the hours in a state of constant arousal, until you are so out of your mind with wanting that you'd take my cock every which way I wanted to give it to you. Where you'd want me to tear into your pussy, fuck your arse, take me down that gorgeous throat of yours. Where you'd want me to use you any way I desire. Where you'd be nothing but my little fuck toy, to wrench every last pleasure from your body until you are delirious and ready to climax over and over again...only..."

"Only?" She whispers.

"Only I wouldn't let you come."

I release her and she shudders.

I rise to my feet, then jerk my chin toward her bedroom door. "Go."

12

Ava

"What do you mean, go?" I stare at him.

"It's English. You do understand English, don't you?"

He sits down on the couch, then lies back and closes his eyes.

The bastard closes his eyes, as if this is the end of the discussion. Finish. Over. Kaput. What in the ever-lovin' hell is wrong with him? I jump up to my feet. "What do you think you're doing?"

Asshole simply folds his hands behind his neck. His biceps bulge and the planes of his chest undulate. Why the hell does he have to be so hot? Why does he have to be so damn obnoxious? And all those filthy things he said… I don't want him to do that to me… I don't…. Do I? And that dream… What the hell was that about? My subconscious playing tricks on me? Trying to justify why I should let Baron fuck me…when my heart still belongs to Edward. Does it belong to Edward?

I'd known him for such a short period of time. Had barely gotten to know him as a person. You don't need that to know though. When you know, you know…right? That's how Bella had known about Edward from the first moment she'd seen him. And then there was Jacob. Shit, I'd always been obsessed with Edward but a part of me had always wanted Jacob. I'd veered toward Edward because he'd been larger-than-life, all consuming. And…I'd always thought I had to choose. In which case, it was Edward. No brainer. But what if I didn't have to choose. What if… I could have both. First Edward… Then Jacob?

Jesus, I am a slut. That much is clear. And that…is all fiction. This is real life. Where the man I'd fallen for had walked out on me and now there is another man—a hot, sexy, beautifully-sculpted alphahole who is sprawled out on my couch, wearing only a pair of briefs, which ride low on his waist. I drag my gaze down the tented center of his crotch—is that an ongoing phenomenon or just something he sports when around me? And he is attracted to me… Clearly. Which is why he had lashed out at me.

"I know what you are doing," I mutter.

"Oh?" His voice is bored.

"You think you can scare me away by putting all of your thoughts into words? You think you can paint the filthiest picture possible in the hope that it would make me think twice about wanting to be with you? Well, you thought wrong."

"Is that what you think I was doing?" He brings up his other hand to scratch his chest and I shiver. My nerve endings pop. I can't take my gaze off of how he drags his fingertips down his sculpted pecs. Goosebumps rise on my skin. I squeeze my thighs together.

"I know that's what you were doing."

"Go to bed, Ava," he drawls. "You don't want to play with things you have no idea about."

"Then teach me."

He freezes. "Excuse me?"

"You heard me." I walk over to the sofa on my knees. "It's why Edward asked you to take care of me."

He lowers his arm to the side. "You think Edward wanted me to fuck you?"

"Didn't he?"

He glares at me. "You're not thinking straight."

"No, you're not thinking straight." I rise to my feet. "Why would he ask you to watch over me in his absence if it weren't for the fact that he knew you'd be attracted to me?"

"Precisely," he mutters. "He knew I'd be attracted to you, but that I'd never go back on my promise to him."

"What promise?" I frown. "What did he make you promise?"

Baron looks at me then glances away.

Ed wouldn't, would he? "Tell me, Baron," I insist, "what did Edward ask you to promise?"

Baron rubs the back of his neck and a dull headache pounds at my temples, "He asked you not to fuck me, am I right?" I say in a low voice. "He asked you to look after me but not fuck me."

Baron blows out a breath, then straightens his shoulders. "Yeah," he mutters, "he explicitly asked me not to approach you. I was supposed to watch over you, but not reveal my presence."

"But you did."

"And here I am." Baron's lips twist.

"And that's not the first promise you have broken."

His brows draw down. "What was that?"

"I said," I squeeze my fingers together, "that it's not like you've kept all of your promises to him."

"What are you talking about?"

"Uh... You and Edward," I mumble. "Surely, you must have broken your promise to him and the rest of the Seven when you left for the army, so it's not like he'd have expected you to keep this promise. In fact, I'd wager that he fully expected you to break it. Which is why he trusted you to watch over me."

"That's the word though, isn't it? Trust." He sets his jaw. "I am not about to break my word."

"No, but you'll do everything in your power to ensure that I break mine." Not that I had promised anything to Edward, but surely, it is in a rule book somewhere the you can't sleep with a man and then with his best friend/enemy... Or whatever they are to each other...right?

"You're not making any sense." He frowns.

"You're the one not making sense." I throw up my hands. "First, you make me come…"

"I didn't touch you."

"A technicality." I huff. "You made me orgasm through my clothes. It's the same thing."

He drags his gaze down to my core, and his nostrils flare. "Trust me, it's not."

My knees tremble. "Then you throw that filthy dialogue at me, arouse me to fever pitch, then you expect me to walk inside and go to sleep."

"Sounds about right," he grumbles.

"Do you know how…how…frustrated I am right now?"

"That makes two of us," he groans.

"So why can't you just…just…put us both out of this misery?"

"Because," his voice takes on a long-suffering tone, "it's not right."

"Since when do you care about what's right and wrong, huh?"

"Since," his throat moves as he swallows, "since I made the decision to come home."

Home. This city is his home. The Seven are his family and Edward is his friend… And me? What am I in all this? Who am I to Edward? To him? Why do I feel so torn between them when, really, neither of them has done anything to stake his claim on me, or said anything to make me feel that I am special? Well, Edward had. Both when he'd fucked me and in my dreams. And Baron… He's shown through his actions that he feels something for me. But none of that is enough, is it? I need more. I deserve to be shown that I matter… That I am special and important enough for them to change things for me. That they want me more than anything in the world. And until then… I belong to neither. I belong to myself, first and foremost. I can do anything I want, and fuck what either of them thinks about it.

"So, you are here to take care of me, right?"

"Right."

"And watch over me?"

"Mmm…hmmm." He yawns.

"And ensure nothing happens to me?"

He nods slowly.

"And you are not going to touch me because you feel like you owe Edward something?"

A line appears between his eyebrows. "Your point being?"

"Just setting the parameters, that's all." I pivot on my heel and walk toward my bedroom, aware that he's watching my every step.

I give an extra twitch of my butt and hear his sharp inhale. Good. Two can play this game... Or three... Doesn't matter. What's clear is that I am not going to let either of them fuck around with me. I am my own woman. I am strong and independent and worked my ass off to get where I am. It's time I behave like one.

I reach the doorway to my bedroom, then turn. "Goodnight, Baron."

He glares back.

Jerk! Seriously, someone needs to remove that stick, or whatever it is, stuck up his arse.

I step through the door, close it gently, then show him the finger.

"I saw that."

His voice reaches me and I glower at him. *Ass.* I stick out my tongue, then pivot and head for my bed. I fling myself on it. I must have been more tired than I thought because the next thing I know, it's morning.

I roll out of bed, shrug on my pajamas, then stumble out into the living room. The couch is empty, the cover folded neatly and placed across the pillow. Apparently, that military training is good for something. I walk into the kitchen and the scent of coffee greets me. I go to the coffee maker, pour myself a cup and take a sip. Yum! The man knows how to make coffee.

I walk toward it, place my cup of coffee on the counter and pick up the folded note next to it. The words leap off the paper.

Don't skip your breakfast.

· · ·

Gah! What the hell? That's it? He didn't even sign it. I mean, there isn't anyone else here who could have left it. But still. I crumple up the paper and am about to throw it away. Instead, I sink down into the chair, smooth it out and stare at the words as I eat.

He'd cooked me an omelet… Still warm. Which means he hadn't left too long ago. How had I not heard him leave? Though, to be fair, once I fall asleep, it's always difficult to wake me up. Had he peeked in on me before he left? Shit, I have to stop that particular fantasy of mine. It's creepy if someone watches you as you sleep. Even more so if it's a man… A hot, sexy, deliciously yummy man with a lot of issues. Boy, does he have issues. Is that why I am attracted to him?

First Edward, now Baron. Between the number of issues, the two of them have, they could keep all the psychologists in London busy. At least, one of them could cook. I finish off the omelet, then drain my cup of coffee. And it isn't because he commanded me to eat. Nope… Nah… I stare at the paper again. Will he return again to use the couch this evening? I hope so. It's the only way I can put the plan I have into action.

Rising, I wash my dishes at the sink, then head for my bedroom. Picking up my phone, I dial Isla's number.

Baron

I'd followed Ava as she'd headed from the tube station to her dance studio. Across from me, a couple of boys walked by, smoking. As I watched, one of them kicked the door that led to the dance studio. I pushed open the car door, but by the time I'd rounded the car, they'd already taken off. I'd glanced up and down the road and found no other cars or people. Which isn't unusual in this part of London. Not that London isn't a safe place, in general, but this is one of the shabby chic parts of the East End. It is up and coming, but still rough in parts. Many of the buildings have been converted to either offices or the kind of loft apartments that sell for millions. The remaining apartments are low-cost council housing. There's nothing in between. The extremes are what makes it dangerous.

It's why I'd asked Ava, once again, to move her studio somewhere safer, but she'd declined. Serves me right. I had insulted her pride when I'd criticized her studio, and in front of her friend. Of course, she's not going to back down about it now. Woman is stubborn. It leaves me no choice but to ensure I watch over her as closely as possible to secure her safety. But she is inside the building now. Which means she won't emerge until late evening, once her classes are completed. Luckily, Ava is a creature of habit. I could set my clock by her.

Is she as habitual when it comes to men? Is she as loyal? Does she still have feelings for Edward? Shit. I drag my fingers through my hair. Standing in the middle of the road, contemplating their relationship isn't helping me at all. Nor had the filthy words that I'd spoken to her last night—which, as she'd guessed, I'd done for effect...in the hope of scaring her off. Not that it had worked. It had only served to get her back up. She'd marched into her bedroom, leaving me with a raging boner... One which I'd been sporting since I'd made her come. Fuck. When she'd come apart on my tongue... I swear, I could taste her cum through the fabric of her leggings...and her panties. Assuming she'd been wearing panties... Were they the same ones she'd been wearing when I'd sprung up from my sleep and taken her down?

I could have seriously hurt her... Fuck... See? That's the reason I've imposed this restraint on myself. No, I am doing the right thing keeping away from her. So, why am I still standing here watching the window of her studio like a schmuck? She'll be safe there for a few more hours. I can use that time to pound the frustration out of my system.

I turn back to the SUV, climb inside and ease onto the road. In half an hour, I've reached my destination.

Grabbing my gym bag from the back of the car, I head inside the building. Situated right next to the Dorchester Hotel, in the center of the city, it's prime real estate. If it were converted to flats, it likely would fetch an annual income equivalent to the GDP of a small third-world country. But Jace, the owner and a friend of the Seven, prefers to keep the gym inside intact.

When he'd learned that I'm back in town, he'd reached out to me and offered me the use of the gym, which I had gladly accepted.

I walk up the steps and into the large room with the boxing ring in the center. Walking into the dressing room, I emerge a few minutes later clad in shorts and a T-shirt. Binding my hands, I pull on my boxing gloves and head for the punching bag. I swing at the bag, punch it again and again. Ten minutes in, I am panting. Sweat beads my upper body, my forehead, and my T-shirt sticks to my skin. I take a break, wipe the sweat from my face. Raise my fists again, when footsteps sound.

"Want to go a round?"

I stiffen, turn around to find Sinner standing behind me.

"With you?" I scoff.

"Scared I'll whip your arse?" he taunts.

I shake my head. "You arrogant twat." I nod toward his office wear. "You going to change out of your pretty boy clothes?"

"No need." He walks to where a chair is positioned next to the ring. Shrugging off his jacket, he hangs it across the back of the chair, then unbuttons his cuffs and pulls off his shirt. I walk over to the ring and climb in, wait for Sinclair to join me.

The squeak of shoes on the flooring warns me about the arrival of the others.

Weston ambles in, followed by Damian, Arpad, and a guy I don't recognize.

Sinclair binds his hands, then steps into the ring as he pulls on his gloves. He rolls his shoulders, bounces around on the balls of his feet as he takes position.

"Who's the new guy?" I ask.

He glances over his shoulder, then turns back to me. "Liam Kincaid."

"Any relation to Weston?"

"His brother. He's also the second richest man in the UK," he mutters.

"Who's the first?"

He scowls back at me and I raise my hands. "That would be you, I take it?"

He smirks. "So, what are you wagering?"

"Wasn't aware this was that type of a fight."

"I only fight for high stakes, and you know that."

"Hmm." I smack my gloved hands together. "If I win, you let go of whatever grudge it is you hold against me."

"And if you lose?"

"I won't try to get back in with the Seven again."

He tilts his head, then nods. "Deal."

I take my stance, when he straightens again. "Hang on, we need a referee." He turns and calls out, "Liam, care to referee our fight here?"

Liam prowls forward. "You're aware I won't do you any favors?"

"Wouldn't expect anything less." Sinclair bares his teeth. Liam nods. He struts over, springs onto the platform in a lithe move that belies his size, then ducks inside the ring.

"And you are?" He turns to me.

"Baron." I jerk my chin at him, and he turns to Sinclair.

"You sure you want to take him on? He seems in much better shape than you."

Sinclair scowls. "Just stick to your allocated role."

He twists his lips, then steps back.

Sinclair and I face each other.

"I let you off too lightly the last time," he mutters.

"Bullshit." I roll my shoulders. "We had polite company watching, so I spared you. This time, it's no holds barred, asshole." I spring forward and bury my fist in his stomach. The breath rushes out of him. He stumbles back, only to recover as I swipe my fist forward. He ducks, swiping at me. I lean aside and his fist slides past my face. I aim for his solar plexus, but he swings first and catches me in the shoulder. The same shoulder he hit yesterday. Motherfucker. Pain sizzles up my spine; I shove it aside, aim for his forehead, connect. His head snaps back. I follow up with an uppercut. He evades me, lands his fist in my side. My ribs protest as sparks flash behind my eyes. Fuck me. I move back, circle, and he does the same. We move at the same time. Clash in the center, chest to chest, arms wrapped around each other. Forehead to forehead.

"Give up," he growls.

"Never." One arm locked around his shoulder, I aim for his ribs, but can't get a hit in, as he continuously keeps moving...and me with him. We stay locked in the dance, trying to hit each other, failing, holding each other's gaze. No way, am I going to blink first. Neither will he. Shit. He grabs the backs of my shoulders, thrusting his face into mine. "Give in."

"No fucking way," I snarl, pulling free, land a hit in his side, then I kick his legs out from under him. He falls on his back, and I follow him down on one knee, pressing my gloved hand against his windpipe.

The referee whistles.

I ignore it, bare my teeth at Sinner.

"You cheated," he snaps out.

"All's fair in war. You were the one who taught me that, remember?"

"Is this war?" He raises an eyebrow.

I scowl down at him, then release him and rise to my feet.

"You two were only trying to kill each other, I take it?" Liam drawls.

"How did you guess?" I smirk, then turn and hold out my hand.

Sinner stares at it for a second, before reaching out and grasping it. I haul him up to his feet. We scowl at each other for a second, then he nods. "Good fight."

"Yeah," I glance down at his Italian loafers, "next time you should wear the right footwear. It makes a difference."

"You always did prefer to follow the rules," he muses.

"Yeah." I blow out a breath. "It's why I joined the army."

"And how did that turn out for you?"

"I've seen better."

"Me too." Sinclair's lips twitch.

"Your fighting skills have improved," I mutter.

"Yours haven't." He smirks.

"I've been busy recovering from the aftermath of—"

He nods. "When we found out you had been taken again..." he shakes his head, "it fucking cut us to the bone."

I squeeze my eyes shut. "Me too, bro. Me too."

"I assume this little demonstration was to show me just how loyal you are to your partners?" Liam interjects. "If so, consider the message received."

Sinclair nods. "You're Weston's brother, which means, there's a connection of trust which I won't breach."

"You guys done fighting?" Weston calls out from below.

I duck under the ropes, then jump down, "We're done *talking*," I retort. "And I need to get out of here, else I'll be late."

"You still on babysitting duties?" He quirks an eyebrow.

"What's it to you?" I scowl.

He pulls out a phone, swipes the screen and hands it over to me.

I stare at the phone, then stiffen. The video shows a woman dressed in a sleeveless red dress that contrasts with her pale skin and matches the red of her lips. She throws back her head and laughs at something that her companion...a man in a suit who's seated opposite her says.

The hair on the back of my neck rises. For a second there... in profile, she'd resembled my mystery girl. The one I'd spotted on the train platform a few years ago as she had thrown her head back and laughed at something that her sister had said. Goosebumps pop on my skin. Shit, this obsession with that red-haired woman of my dreams is definitely going to make me do something I am going to regret.

She tilts her head and her hair catches the light and burnished copper glints back at me. Her cheeks are rosy and her green eyes sparkle. She's, clearly, enjoying herself.

"Motherfucker," I growl. "Who sent this to you?"

"Amelie." He tilts his head. "She spotted Ava at the restaurant... which, luckily, happens to be next door."

"Next door?" I frown. "At the Dorchester?"

He nods and I brush past him, heading for the exit.

"You may want to change," he calls out.

I pause, glance down at my gym shorts and T-shirt. I'm sweaty, but who cares? Maybe she would? And if I stay to shower, no telling what the douche in a suit might get up to in that time.

Damian ambles over to us. "I know you're thinking it doesn't matter, but you don't want to be turning up there dressed like this."

"Like what?"

"Like a desperate asshole who interrupted his gym session to break up her date."

"I'm going to smash his head in," I interrupt him, "but that's beside the point."

"Aren't you getting a little too…possessive, here."

"So?"

"She's not yours. You know that, right?"

"Of course, I do," I say through gritted teeth. "I'm merely doing what Edward would have done in my place."

"That's all it is?" Sinner draws closer.

"Yes."

"You sure?" Weston asks.

"The fuck you guys care?"

"We care about you, bro," Damian says softly. "You've forgotten that when you are part of the Seven, you get all of us in your corner."

"That include Saint?" I mutter.

"Saint." Sinclair blows out a breath. "He's still pissed at you."

"What's his issue?" I rub the back of my neck. "You'd think I did something to personally anger him."

"Of the lot of us, he's the most sentimental," Weston offers.

"Saint." I stare at him. "You're joking, right?"

Weston holds my gaze, then smirks.

"You *are* joking." I roll my shoulders. "You had me there, for a second, Wes. I'd forgotten just how good an actor you are."

"We haven't forgotten what you've been through," Damian retorts. "You could have reached out to us when you were released. You could have come home."

"I came now."

"After that asshole, Edward, found a way to get you back," Sinclair declares.

I scowl. "Wait. Hold on. Edward didn't do anything. I came back of my own volition."

"After he told you he needed your help," Weston reminds me.

"Wait, so you all think it was an elaborate plan on his part to get me here?"

"Maybe he killed two birds with one stone." Damian lifts his shoulders.

"He always was the most strategic of the lot of us." Sinclair rubs his jaw.

Liam draws abreast. "It was fun while it lasted but...I have to get going."

"Oh?" Sinclair asks, "Important date?"

"A wedding rehearsal."

"You mean your wedding rehearsal, don't you?" Weston pipes up, and Liam shoots him a dirty glare.

"See you later, *little* brother."

He stalks out.

"Why do I get the feeling he's not happy about his upcoming nuptials?" Damian stares after him.

"Because he isn't?" Weston suggests.

"So why go through with it?"

"Inheritance." Weston shrugs. "What can I say? We one-percenters find all the possible ways to make it complicated for our offspring to live their lives. In this case, if older brother, here, doesn't get married and produce an heir soon, he doesn't get access to the family business nor to his trust fund."

I wince. "Complicated."

"You're telling me?"

"Good thing I don't have such issues."

"You don't have an empire to inherit, either," Damian reminds me.

"I make enough from 7A investments—thanks to you jokers—to not worry about money for a long time," I retort. "Besides, some of us want more than just money."

"Not that old chestnut." Sinclair smirks.

"Speak for yourself, married motherfucker." I scowl.

"Married and soon to be a father," Sinclair declares.

There's silence, then Damian slaps him on the back.

Weston grips his shoulder. "Congratulations, bro!"

A hot sensation stabs in my chest. What the hell? Why am I jealous of what he has? I made a choice, remember? Besides, I'd never be safe with any woman. Remember what happened just last night?

I reach forward, hold out my hand and Sinclair shakes it. "Congratulations," I mutter. "I am happy for you."

Sinclair grins, and that throws me. Jesus, in all the time I've known him since the incident, he's never seemed this happy. Is that what being married to the right woman does to you? Makes you more human?

Can I afford to be more human? Can I allow myself to feel the gamut of emotions that comes with being with the right woman? Hell, I know the answer to that. I may have found her, but I am not right for her. I can't jeopardize her safety any more than I already have. I need to stick to my promise, ensure that she is okay, keep her safe until Edward returns.

I turn, head for the shower. "Give me five minutes."

"It's not that I'm a social recluse and never had any friends. And it's true that sometimes I prefer staying home on a Friday night with a good book and a hot chocolate; that doesn't mean that the only reason that I had imaginary friends was because I felt lonely..."
-From Ava's Diary

Ava

"So, you're a dancer?"

The man on the other side of the table leans forward. His gaze takes me in and his eyes light up appreciatively.

"Uh, yeah. I am a dance instructor and I also have set pieces I perform at events, and on stage."

"Unusual profession."

"Nothing wrong with being a dancer," I say stiffly.

"Of course, not." He holds up his hands. "It was just a comment. I am sorry if I offended you."

I blow out a breath. *Come on, you can try to be civil. It's not his fault that he's not Baron...or Edward.* I shake my head, tip up my chin.

"And you?" I frown into his muddy brown eyes. "What do you do again, Calvin?"

"It's Kevin." He frowns.

"Kevin," I correct myself, "sorry. You said you work in an office, right?" Not that I remember, but what are the chances he doesn't.

"Actually, I am a fireman."

"A fireman?" I glance at him closely. His dark hair is pushed back from his face, his eyes are intelligent, his chin shaved, and he's wearing a shirt, that outlines the breadth of his shoulders which, although not as impressive as Baron's (or Edward's), are decent enough to indicate that he does not, in fact, spend all of his time behind a desk.

"So, you fight fires?" I murmur.

"That's what firemen are known to do, yes." He grins and his eyes twinkle. Actually, they are not a muddy brown as much as a gray brown. Nowhere near the amber of another man. A man whom I had met and lost in such a short period of time that I am beginning to wonder if he'd been a figment of my imagination. Then I look at Baron and I know he isn't. Baron's a reminder of the Seven, and that includes Edward...

So yeah, he'd definitely been real. I only have to tune into my body to remember how he'd possessed me. How he'd taken me and imprinted himself into every cell of my body in such a short period of time. I squeeze my finger around the stem of my wine glass so hard that the ruby red liquid spills out. The stain blots the white table cloth and I swallow. Tears prick the backs of my eyes. Damn it, what is wrong with me, that such a small incident is pushing me over the edge? Bloody Baron. It's all his fault that I am strung so tight. It's because of him that I am here, faking interest in a man—who, to be honest, isn't all that bad looking, or boring, coming to think of it. He isn't Edward or Baron, though.

"You okay?" His voice cuts through my thoughts.

I glance up at him and shake my head. "Yeah, sorry, been a long few days."

"Want to talk about it?" The lines around his eyes deepen. He really is good-looking. Too bad he isn't either of the men who are currently on my mind. Men? Did I just think men? Why the hell am I thinking of them in the plural? Edward is gone; Baron is here. If anything, it's only Baron I should be thinking of right now. Or should I? Is it healthy to switch from one man to the other so quickly? I drag my fingers through my hair. This entire situation is getting out of hand. I rise to my feet, and he rises with me. "Everything all right?"

"Y…yeah." I swallow, "Just going to the restroom."

"You sure you're fine?"

"Yes," I force my lips to curve, "I'll be right back."

I head past the other diners—couples, families—all eating, enjoying themselves on a night out before they go home to their lives, their safety nets, their little corners of the world filled with love and happiness.

And me? What about me? What have I done, except screw up every single thing in my life? I'd had the chance to become a doctor and had dropped out. Then, I'd met Edward, and instead of turning away, I'd headed for the one thing I'd known I could never have. And then Baron. What the hell am I even doing, planning this entire charade…for his benefit? Why couldn't I simply *not* act on my impulses this time? Why can't I have a normal, safe, boring life? Because I am an idiot. Because I'll never be content with a life where I don't truly feel. Because I have to be fully engaged in everything I do. Because I can't live half a life. Because I have to be true to myself, and to what I want, no matter that it's unconventional. No matter if it is not how things are done in the rest of the world. Because…

I want him. As much as I want Edward. There, I've said it. Well, I've thought it. I walk into the restroom, reach the sink and grip the edge. I stare at myself in the mirror. The pale cheeks, the lipstick almost bitten off, my hair about my shoulders. "Why…why do you always have to go after what you can't have? Why do you have to be different? Why can't you be…normal?"

"Because you could try to hide in a crowd, and yet, you'd always stand out."

I whip my head around to find Baron stepping into the restroom.

"Because you are a shining star in the night sky." He meets my gaze, and his jaw tics. "Because you're the one unbroken seashell on the shore." He folds his arms across his chest. "And I am not going to let you walk out of here until you admit that you set up this scene to get my attention."

I straighten, fold my arms and mirror his stance. "G…get out." Shit, why am I stuttering? I am not nervous. I am not. I square my shoulders, scowl at his reflection in the mirror. "This is the ladies' room," I insist. "You shouldn't be here."

He bares his teeth. "This is exactly where I need to be."

I huff, "I am with someone else." I hold his gaze. "He's out there waiting for me."

"So, what are you doing here?"

I reach for the paper towels, pretend to dry my hands. "I was just leaving, actually." I turn and march up to the door, but of course, he doesn't move.

"Get out of the way," I hiss.

"Not until you tell me what you want."

"What I want," I flip my hair over my shoulder, "is for you to leave me alone."

"Funny, from where I am," he looks me up and down, "it seems like quite the opposite."

"Your ego is showing," I snap.

"And you," he widens his stance, "are lying."

"No."

"Yes."

"Let me go."

"No."

"Why are you doing this?"

"Me?" He glares at me. "I'm not the one pretending to be on a date in order to draw attention to myself."

I gape at him. "You have some nerve…you…you asshole."

"Alphahole." His grin widens. "I prefer alphahole."

"What-bloody-ever." I huff, "If you don't get out of my way, I'll…"

"What, what will you do?"

"I'll scream."

"No, you won't."

I gape at him, open my mouth…then shut it. "Damn you," I hiss. "Why did you have to come back and spoil everything?"

His jaw tightens, then he flexes his shoulders. "Your insults do nothing to me."

"So, what are you doing here then?"

"Making sure you don't do anything that you'll regret later."

"What do you mean?" I scowl.

"Your date. Ditch him."

My jaw drops. "What the hell? If you think you can rule my life —"

"Think?" He looks me up and down. "I have news for you, I already do."

"No, you don't."

"Yes, I do."

"You…you have no claim on me."

"Edward does."

"He lost any rights when he left."

"He had his reasons."

I clench my fists at my sides, "Oh, so now you're defending him?"

"Only because he's not here to do it himself." He shuffles his feet. "Look…just...do as I say and we can pretend this never happened."

"You mean, I should pretend that you didn't just come marching in here like a rhinoceros —"

"Rhinoceros?"

"Okay, alphaceros."

"First time I've been called that… Whatever that is."

I draw in a breath, try to clear my head. "Just… Let me walk out of here, and we can forget this ever happened."

"Nope." He smirks.

My jaw drops, "Seriously, you're a piece of work."

"I aim to impress."

"Far from," I scoff.

"You don't know it yet, but you are," his grin widens, "impressed."

"No, I'm not." I scowl at him. "And you're fooling yourself if you think otherwise."

The smile fades from his face. He peers into my eyes, and his gaze intensifies, "It's too late," he mutters, almost to himself. "I did meet you, and now I can't get you out of my head."

"Wh…what do you mean?" I swallow. "What are you trying to say?"

"You heard me." His eyes gleam. "You set up this entire charade, knowing it would get to me, didn't you?"

"N…no."

"Yes, you did. Admit it."

"I'll do no such thing." I firm my lips. "What I do with my life is of no consequence to you."

"You're right."

"I am?"

He nods. "Everything you do is not just of consequence, but it affects me. Since I saw you, I can't stop thinking of you. Everywhere I look, I see you. Every time I get a whiff of jasmine, images of you, your curves, your sweet tits, the way your cunt responds to my ministrations—all of it overcomes me."

"Oh," I breathe, "wh…what are you trying to say?"

"That I should give into this overwhelming need to throw you down and take you, but—"

"But you won't." I complete the statement for him.

He nods.

"Then let me out."

"Doesn't mean I can't make you come again."

14

Ava

"Wh…what?" He moves forward and I skitter back. "What do you mean?"

"What I said earlier."

"You…can't be serious."

"Don't pretend you didn't enjoy it the last time."

"So, what if I did?" I jut out my chin. "Doesn't mean I want it again."

"Don't you?" His eyes gleam as if he's enjoying a private joke.

"Asshole."

"Told you, I prefer alphahole."

"And I prefer…that you step aside and let me pass."

"Not happening." He takes another step in my direction. I slide back until my hip touches the washbasin.

"Turn around, grip the edge of the sink," he says.

"No." I set my jaw.

"Oh?" He reaches out, circles my throat, his grip gentle… Too gentle. I need him to curl those thick fingers around my nape, to hold me down as he shoves aside my panties and plants his swollen dick inside me... Like Edward did. Jesus, I need to stop thinking of both of them in the same breath, same vision, same time. No, no, no.

His grasp intensifies, and goosebumps pop on my skin.

"Don't," I swallow, "don't do it."

"Say 'no' one more time, and I'll step back. I'll leave here and walk out and you'll never see me again."

Say it. Do it. It's what you want, right? I'd staged this entire charade for his benefit and now, when he is here and finally intent on giving me physical pleasure—again, I am losing my nerve. Damn it, what's happening to me? Do I want him to leave? And then...what? He returns to keeping vigil in his car? And I see him when I bring him coffee? And he follows me home every night, interrupts my dates like this, threatens to give me an orgasm, without ever committing to me? Do I want him to commit to me...when my heart still belongs to Edward? Is this the way forward? To allow myself some level of physical comfort with him? Allow him to pleasure me, to use my body, to fill my thoughts and my mind with his touch, his scent, his nearness, so that, temporarily at least, I can forget about how it could have been with Edward?

"Fine," I whisper.

"Fine?"

I nod. I bring my hands up to grip his wrist, the circumference so thick that my fingers barely meet around it. "I...I'll do as you ask."

His gaze intensifies, then he jerks his chin. He releases me, only to grasp my waist and turn me like we were in some kind of dance. I face his reflection in the mirror.

"Bend over."

Before I can comply, he kicks my legs apart.

I squeak. He presses his wide palm into the center of my back and pushes down. I comply and a breath whooshes out of him. "My god, Eve, you should look at yourself."

"Wh...what did you call me?"

"Hmm?" He drags his fingers down to cup my arse and all

thoughts leak from my head. Moisture pools in my center and my toes curl.

"This dress?" He swipes his hand down my thigh, until it grazes the hem. "I fucking hate it."

"It's a perfectly nice dress," I protest.

"And you wore it for another man."

"You have no claim on me."

"I am the one protecting you."

"From what?" I mutter, "Likely, imaginary enemies who are a figment of your imagination—"

His hand connects with my backside and I gasp. "What the hell?"

"Shh!" He slaps my right arse cheek, then the left, and the right, so rapidly that I forget to scream. Forget to protest, forget to do anything else but focus on the heat that pools between my legs. Jesus. I am soaked, and all he's done is spank me. What the hell is wrong with me, that I crave how he hurts me? How he anchors me with his hold on my pussy as he slides his hand around and grips me between my legs. I moan and behind me he goes rigid. "You like this." His voice lowers to a hush. He yanks my dress up around my waist, then pushes aside my panties and shoves his fingers inside my cunt.

"Baron," I groan, "Omigod, Baron."

"Yeah, that's it, baby. Just like that," he croons as he begins to work his fingers in and out of me. In and out. In and out.

My belly clenches; my thighs tremble. A bead of sweat works its way down my temple. "Oh!" I whine. "Please, please."

"What do you want, baby?" He grabs my hair and tugs it back with enough force that my scalp protests. Pain slithers down my spine, arrowing straight to that groaning, growling, emptiness deep inside of me that stutters and coils in on itself.

"Please." I gulp, "Please make it stop."

"Like this?" He pulls his fingers out of me, only to reach back and tear my panties off.

"O-Oh." I stutter.

"How many more ways can you say, 'Oh'... Shall we find out?"

He releases his grip on my hair, and before I can turn around, he's dropped down to his knees between my legs. He shoves his face between my thighs, licks my slit, all the way up to between my arse cheeks.

"Ohh," I moan, "Ohhh, Baron."

I sense his lips curve against my sensitive skin, a second before he grabs my arse cheeks and squeezes them apart. Pain vibrates out from the point of contact and my core seems to melt. I grip the edge of the sink, push out my butt and lower my forehead to the cool ceramic surface.

He swipes his tongue up my pussy, thrusts his tongue inside my melting core. At the same time, he slides his thumb inside my puckered hole and I squeal. "Oh, no, no, no, no."

He pauses, "Is that a yes, Eve?"

I hesitate, then nod.

"Say it."

"Yes."

"Like you mean it, Eve," he orders.

"Yes, you bastard," I huff, "you alphahole, you—"

He bites down on my pussy and I cry out. He curves his thumb inside my back channel, as he brings his fingers up to pinch on my clit. The climax screams up my legs, and that's when someone knocks on the door.

He pulls his fingers and his tongue out of me, and the orgasm recedes.

"No!" I yell.

"Is that a no, darlin'?"

"No," I growl, "you sadist, it's not."

"Then what is it?"

"If you don't make me come in the next five seconds—"

Someone bangs on the door, then a woman's voice yells, "Customers need to use the restroom, can you—?"

"NO," I yell, "go away!"

"But—" the woman protests.

"I'll be out in—" I stare at the jerkass from the corner of my eyes, "three—" He raises his eyebrows. "Five minutes."

"I'll have to call security ma'am."

"You do what you have to do," I retort. "Just go away, now."

The steps recede, and I level my gaze on him, "If you don't put your mouth on me —"

He shoves his tongue inside my channel, grinds his heel into my clit and the breath whooshes out of me.

"Omigod. Omigod."

He works his tongue in and out of me, then slides his fingers up to strum my pussy lips; at the same time, he slides his finger, no, two fingers, inside my backchannel and I explode. The orgasm crashes through me and I cry out. Tendrils of heat flare out from where he continues to eat me out. Continues to worry my clit, to squeeze the swollen nub, which sends another shudder racing through me. After-shocks of pleasure-pain grip me, and I slump. He rises to his feet and catches me, turns me around, rights my clothes. He leans forward until our eyelashes tangle and I am sure that he is going to kiss me. Instead, he pats my cheek. "Next time I'll make you come in 60 seconds."

He turns to leave and I blink. *Wait, what?* What was that about? He reaches the door, twists the handle to open it.

"What the hell do you mean by that?"

"Exactly what you heard, babe." He half turns his head to fix me with his gaze. "Assuming there's a next time, of course."

Turning, he leaves.

15

Ava

I run out of the door, watch as he disappears up the corridor, toward what I assume is the back door of the restaurant. I step toward him, when someone grips my arm.

"Are you okay?"

I jerk my head around to find Calvin—I mean, Kevin—holding my elbow. I glance down at where his fingers press into my skin, then up at him. Instantly, he releases me and steps back. "I came to give you this." He holds out my handbag and jacket.

"Oh," I take the jacket, shrug into it, then grab my bag, "thank you, I was coming back—"

"No, you weren't."

No, I wasn't. And maybe I should be embarrassed about it, but to hell with that. I am not going to regret my actions. I tip up my chin, meet his gaze.

"It's okay," he holds up his hands, "I know you're with someone else."

"No, I'm not."

"Hmm." He raises his shoulders. "If you say so."

"Look," I blow out a breath, "it's just that you aren't—"

"Him." Kevin jerks his chin toward the backdoor.

"Y…yeah," I mumble. "You're a good man, Kevin. It's just…" I shake my head. "Sorry, I should have never agreed to this date."

"Hey," he half smiles. "at least, now I know what it means to be in love."

"I'm not in love—"

He shakes his head, then stabs his thumb at the door. "You'd better catch him before he leaves."

"Yeah." I walk forward, then turn back toward him for a moment. "I truly am sorry." I break into a run, reach the door, shove it open and step out into the chilly, late evening air. Of course, the door leads into an alley. I sprint past the dumpster, past a stool with a cup overflowing with cigarettes. I reach the street, glance in either direction, don't find any trace of him. Shit, did I lose him? Why did he have to give me such an incredible orgasm then spoil it all with that…that comment about making me come in sixty seconds? My core clenches. Shit, why is it that just thinking about his hands on me, his tongue inside me, his mouth eating me out, turns me on so…so much?

I turn and walk up the street, toward the tube station. A gust of wind blows and I huddle into my coat. I reach the entrance to the subway that leads to the tube station, then hesitate. I glance around me, but there's no one. I pull out my phone and glance at the time. It's only 10pm, not that late. It should be okay, right? I take a step forward, hesitate, then snort. Watching too many movies, that's my problem. It's only a short distance to the tube. I'm sure it's going to be fine. I head down the steps, walk into the subway tunnel.

Footsteps sound behind me. I turn, find no one there. Strange. The hair on the nape of my neck rises. Shit, shit, shit, why had I not obeyed my instincts? Movies are based on real life, after all, and often, fact is stranger than fiction. I break into a run, heading for the steps that lead onto the platform of the tube station. If I can make it there, I'll be fine. There are bound to be tube staff around, not to mention, other passengers.

I just need to get down the next set of stairs and— A man bounds up the steps, wearing a black suit with black loafers. What the hell, is he a commuter?

Then, he plants himself in my path and I know he's not. I stop so suddenly that I stumble. Footsteps approach me from behind. I swing around to find there are two men closing in on me from the other side. Both are dressed in suits in varying shades of black. Shit, what is this? Who are these guys? I turn, back up, take a step back, another. The first man I'd seen moves toward me and I stumble back. My hip grazes the wall and a scream tumbles from my lips. "Who… who are you?" I reach for my bag, hold it out in front of me like a weapon. As if that's going to help.

The man chuckles and the sound echoes around the space. The hair on my forearms rises. My stomach twists in knots. Shit, now I know why villains on screen have an evil laugh. Because they do so in real life, as well.

Shit, this is not good, not good. Someone will be along to help me soon, right?

He takes another step forward and I flatten myself against the wall. "G…get away from me." Shit, why is my voice trembling? If I come across as scared, that will only goad him. I stiffen my shoulders, tip up my chin. "Don't come closer."

I glance around the space, searching for CCTV cameras. There's one in the corner, but it hangs crookedly from the ceiling. Clearly, it's been disconnected. No, no, no, this can't be happening.

The man walks toward me and I cry out, "Come near me and I'll scream."

His grin widens. He reaches me, grabs my shoulder, and I howl. I raise my hand bag and back-hand him across his face. His neck snaps back. He stumbles back, then straightens. Blood drips from his nose. His features twist and he leaps forward, grabs me by my arm, then swings me around with such force that my cheek connects with the hard wall. Lights flash behind my eyes and pain lashes down my spine. My guts twist; the acrid taste of bile fills my mouth. *Fuck. Fuck. Fuck.* Why had I stepped into the subway? Why are these guys attacking me? Where the hell is the jerkass alphahole when I need him? If you're out there, Baron, now would be a good time to show yourself.

My attacker moves closer, presses his body into mine. The scent of something metallic, coated with the greasy smell of burned meat, assails my nose. I gag, try to shake myself free, and something cold pushes into my neck.

"Stop struggling or I'll slit your throat."

I freeze. Try to draw in a breath, but my lungs burn. Shit, shit, shit, what the hell is happening? Am I caught up in a nightmare? He presses the metallic surface—a knife?—into my neck. Pain spirals out from the contact. Drops of something slither down my neck and I know it's blood. OMG, he is going to kill me, he is going to… The man grabs my hip and my heart slams into my chest. No, he is going to do something worse. He is going to— Cool air grazes my back and the scent of pine trees laces my nostrils.

I hear the sound of something smashing into the ground, then the entire tunnel seems to reverberate. I turn, already knowing what I am going to find, and yet, I can't stop the gasp of surprise when I see Baron bring his leg down—hard—into the stomach of the fallen man.

The bastard groans, tries to rise. Baron steps on him, kicks out his other leg to take out another guy, then lunges forward to throw himself at the third. The two go down, roll, hit the opposite wall. The second man he'd hit rises to his feet, attacks him. He grapples while one guy clings to his back, the other in front, who swipes out his fist. Baron swerves and the fist connects with the man behind him. The sound of breaking bones, the *thwap* of knuckles connecting with flesh, then the man yells, lumbering back. The man on the ground stirs and I don't think twice. I stomp my foot squarely on his groin. The guy yells, reaching forward. I step back, kicking him in the shin. The second guy, meanwhile, turns around and lurches for me. I grab my hand bag and swing it up. It connects with his chin and he cries out. He stumbles back, just as Baron throws the third against the wall.

His head connects with the hard surface and he slumps to the ground.

Baron turns, rushes toward the second guy, wraps his hand around his neck, and flings him to the side.

I stumble the other way and Baron brushes past me. He grabs the guy on the ground, hauls him up to his feet and throws him into the wall. "You dare to touch her? You put your hands on her, you motherfucker." He closes his fingers around his face and shoves the back of his head into the wall again and again. The man's body jerks. His eyelids close and his body slumps. Still, Baron doesn't stop. "Bastard. How dare you threaten her? Scum, fucking shitstain of a human, I'm going to kill you, I—"

I jump forward grab his arm. "Stop," I yell, "you are going to kill him!"

Baron shakes me off, his gaze focused on the other guy, "Motherfucker, you dare come near her? I am going to make sure you're never able to touch another woman again."

"Baron!" I scream at him. I throw myself at him, grab his arm and plead with him, "Please, we need to go before someone finds us."

He pauses. His shoulders heave and his breath comes in pants.

"Baron, please, I am tired and—"

He releases the man and turns on me so fast that I blink. He looks me up and down, "Are you wounded?" He closes the distance between us, searches my features. "Did he hurt you?"

"Y...yes," I whisper, "but you hurt me more."

16

Baron

Her lips tremble and her chin wobbles. She squeezes her fingers together, and her knuckles are white. Damn it, I am responsible for this. I allowed my emotions to get the better of me. I walked out of there, left her unprotected for ten minutes, and what happened? They got to her. When I'd seen him put his hands on her, something inside me had detonated. My vision had tunneled; all thoughts had emptied from my head. All I'd known was that he'd touched her. He'd dared to threaten what's mine. She isn't mine. She is…his…but he'd charged me with taking care of her. One simple thing and I had failed. And now…she says I hurt her more than those bastards did? What the fuck?

"How?" I growl, "How did I hurt you?"

"Now you ask?" She tries to shove the hair back from her face but her hand shakes. "You…you walked out on me, you ass. After you made me come. You treated me like I was some kind of…of fuck toy."

"No, I didn't." I wrap my fingers about her throat. "If I had, you wouldn't be standing here mouthing off to me. And after putting yourself at risk."

Her jaw drops and color creeps into her cheeks. Good. At least, she is getting over the shock.

"I put myself at risk?" she hisses at me. "You think I am at fault?"

I nod. "Ever since I saw you, you've crawled under my skin. You've occupied my thoughts, broken through my ability to concentrate. You pushed me to the edge until I had no choice but to walk out on you for your own protection."

"And see how that turned out?" She waves a hand in the air. "Are you happy now?"

I shake my head, apply enough pressure on her throat that her eyes widen. "You are so fucking fragile. I can off you so easily, you'd never even see it coming."

She swallows. "And is that what you want?"

I shake my head again. "I don't know what I want."

"That makes two of us." She shivers and I release my hold on her. I step back, look her up and down, then grip her hand, "Come on, let's get out of here."

I stalk forward, pulling her along. She stumbles, then protests, "Walk slower."

"You need to keep up."

"My legs are shorter than yours, asshole."

"You don't say?" I pause so suddenly she crashes into me. Then, turning, I scoop her up,

"Hey, what the hell? I can walk."

"And see how that turned out?"

She huffs, wriggles around in my arms. I pull her close, her handbag jammed in between us. "Stop it," I growl.

"Or what?"

"Or I'll have to take my hand to your arse when we get to the car."

Her breath hitches. "I'd like to see you do that."

"I'm sure you would." I allow a smirk to curve my lips. "Just as it turns you on to be brought to orgasm with the threat of being discovered in a public place."

"You know nothing," she snaps.

"I know that I am never again letting you go anywhere unguarded."

She freezes, then glances up at me. "Who were those men?"

I set my jaw. If she thinks I am going to tell her anything that could upset her further, she's crazy.

"Don't do that," she snaps, and I stare down at her, before glancing forward again.

"Don't do what?"

"Don't treat me like I am some stupid woman who doesn't know what's happening around her half the time."

"Trust me, if you were, that would make my job so much easier."

"Job?" She raises her voice, "So I am just a job for you, is it?"

Of course, not. Damn her. What the hell does she want me to admit? That from the moment I'd laid eyes on her, this entire plan had been shot to hell? That I should have tasked one of the Seven with protecting her? That I should have turned away and ensured I had nothing to do with her? As if I would have been able to do that. I'll never allow any other man close to her again. And Edward? What about your once best friend? After all, it's thanks to him that you met her. It's because of him that you returned to your life, that you found your life. I tighten my arms and stare ahead of me. "No," I say stiffly, "you're not just a job. You've never been just a job, and you know that."

"Do I?" I sense her stare up at me, but refuse to return her gaze. "Do I know anything about you, Baron?"

"You know enough."

"Spoken like a man," she gripes.

"That's me, all right." I reach the SUV, beeping the doors unlocked as I approach. I lower her to her feet, opening the door for her. She steps in, throws her bag down on the dashboard, then folds her arms across her chest. "You're a jerk."

I bend over her and she freezes. I tug on her seatbelt, snap it into place, then straighten. Her breath catches in her throat; her chest rises and falls. I smirk down at her, "You didn't think I was going to kiss you there, did you?"

"You—" She raises her fist, as I slam the door shut. Good, she's angry. I can work with that. It'll takes her mind off what just happened, while I track down whoever was responsible for that attack, though I have my suspicions. I open my door on the driver's side, then slide in and slam it shut behind me. The entire vehicle rocks.

"What crawled up your pants?" she mutters. "I'm the one who was attacked. If anyone should be angry, it's me."

I turn on her and she meets my gaze head on.

I reach for her, then curl my fingers. "Shut up," I growl. "Not another word out of you."

She sets her jaw, but not before I spot the trembling of her lips. Shit, she is upset. Of course, she's upset and emotional. She was just attacked. I'd let her out of my sight and they'd moved in. If I had been a few seconds later, they'd have hurt her. Anger thrums at my temples and my blood thuds in my veins. I turn, stare forward through the windshield, draw in a breath, another. I can't drive like this. I need to calm down. I rotate my shoulders, glare through the darkness.

"I still don't get why you're so upset."

I move toward her so fast that she squeaks. I thrust my face right into hers. She blinks, skitters back against the window. I follow her until I'm looming over her. She tips up her chin, her green eyes glowing in the darkness. Feline eyes. Eyes of a witch. Of a siren who's entranced me. Who's dug her pretty little claws into me and is hooking me to her in such a way that there is no bloody escape. "You want to know why I'm upset?" I growl. "Want to know why I am so fucking pissed?"

"Y…yes." She nods.

"I'll tell you why I'm so angry that I can't think straight."

I grip her chin and she shudders.

I press down on her lower lip until her mouth opens. Her eyes widen. Color sweeps up her skin. Her chest rises and falls, the nipples puckered and hard and pointing up at me, beckoning to me, beseeching me to squeeze them, tug on them, tweak them so hard that she feels it all the way to the sweet spot between her legs. The soft flesh there contracting, swelling, and filled with heat and wetness, so when I finally take her, I'll slam right into her, up to the hilt. When I finally cram my dick inside her tight little pussy, she'll be ready and willing and open. She'll take all of me, she'll clamp her cunt around my shaft and —

A moan bleeds from her lips and I lower my gaze to her mouth. "Why did you have to be so delectable, so gorgeous, so fucking beautiful, inside and out?"

She swallows. I lower my head and breathe in the exotic perfume of jasmine, and below that, the lush scent of raspberries.

My cock instantly hardens. The blood drains to my groin and my pulse throbs behind my eyelids, at my temples, in my fucking balls. I raise my head and stare into her eyes, "Fuck you, for what you do to me, and fuck me, for what I am going to do to the both of us."

She parts her lips, "What do you — ?"

I close my mouth over hers.

17

Ava

Omigod, his lips are hard and soft at the same time and his tongue... He thrusts it inside my mouth as if he owns it, possesses it, owns me, and in a way, he does. Since he'd hauled me up from my freefall on the sidewalk as I'd watched Edward pull away, and he'd taken care of me and carried me inside the house, I'd known then that I need him. Is that why Edward had asked him to take care of me? Had he known that I'd need him? Since when had I become so dependent on another? I'd had enough courage of conviction to drop out of med school and pursue a career of my own; the kind that most people don't take seriously. And that hadn't bothered me. I had been so sure of myself, knew I had to do it to satisfy that need inside of me that only I felt. The ability to create a dance, to flow with the music, to feel the rhythm in my bones...that...was certainty.

This hot stabbing sensation in my chest, as this man pushes his lips into mine. As he releases my seat belt and pulls me to him, hauls me across the center console of the SUV and onto his lap; as he grips my hips, fits me over his crotch so his hard throbbing shaft settles between my legs? This… I have no idea what to make of it. It had been similar…yet different, with Edward. With him, every encounter had been fraught with tension, and the knowledge that it was forbidden. All of which had only made it even more erotic, more exciting, more real… More everything. With Edward…it had been this sensation that I couldn't resist as he'd drawn me closer, closer within his reach, his pull, his magnetic presence that had floored me, as I'd felt guilty and known that there couldn't possibly be a future between us.

With Baron…the sensations are as strong, and yet, it feels freer, bigger, wider. Like he is larger than life and consuming me, owning me, imprinting his touch into my skin as he wraps his fingers around my throat in a gesture I am coming to recognize as uniquely his.

He presses his thumb down on my chin, forcing me to open my mouth wider, and he angles his head and shoves his tongue across mine. His lips flatten mine, his teeth clash against mine, and suddenly, I am straining against him. I throw my arm around his shoulders, or as much as I can reach, that is. I thrust my breasts into the hard planes of his chest and a groan rumbles from him. He digs his fingers into my hair and tugs. My scalp tingles and heat burns down my spine. My thighs clench and his hard length seems to grow even bigger, thicker, throbbing between us, digging into my soft center as he tilts his head and seems to eat me alive.

"Fuck," he whispers into my mouth and the strength of his intention seems to thicken, deepen until it presses down on the both of us. He tears his mouth from mine, stares up into my eyes. "Jesus, what you do to me, Eve."

"Eve," I clear my throat, "you called me Eve."

"Did I?" He frowns.

I nod. "It's what Edward called me too."

His face hardens and his jaw tics.

"It's just… It's too much of a coincidence that both of you call me by the same nickname, you know?"

A vein pops at his temple, and damn it, so maybe I shouldn't have said it, and definitely I shouldn't have mentioned Edward's name, but the thing is... It really is weird as hell that Baron calls me by the same nickname.

"You have to admit, it's a bit strange?" I prod.

"When Edward called me and asked me to return to watch out for you, he referred to you as Eve. I guess the name must have stuck in my head," he finally says. "Also," his gaze intensifies, "you look like an Eve."

"Oh?" I swallow. "What does an Eve look like?"

"Tempting, luscious, a siren who entrapped me the moment I set eyes on her."

My thighs clench and my toes curl. "O-o-k-a-y," I stutter.

"Is that all you have to say, *Eve?*" He lowers his face, to the junction of where my neck meets my shoulder. He sniffs, drawing in my scent, and something hot unfurls in my belly.

"Sexy Eve. Curvy Eve. Luscious Eve, who I can't wait to get my hands on. I should regret feeling the way I do about you, but you know what?"

"What?" I squeak.

"I don't."

He grabs me about my waist, lifts me back into my seat and I squeak. Whoa, when he handles me like that, like I weigh nothing... It's too sexy, way too much of a turn on. I am way out of my freakin' depth here. He leans over me then snaps my seatbelt into place.

The scent of him fills my senses and my heart begins a slow thump.

I glance away as he starts the car and eases onto the road, all in one smooth move.

We don't talk on the drive home. The silence stretches but neither of us break it.

When we reach my place, he shuts off the engine. We stay that way, wrapped in silence, unable to move, not saying anything to each other. Finally, I turn and push open my door. "Are you coming inside?"

He shoves his door open, walks around and behind me as I reach my front door. I open it, step inside then turn to him. "Those men —"
I swallow.

"They won't hurt you again."

"What if they find me—?"

"They won't."

"How do you know that?"

He glares at me. "I just do."

"Do you know who they are?"

"You don't need to concern yourself with it."

"So, you know who they are?" I glower back at him. "Do they belong to the Mafia or something?"

He sets his jaw, "What makes you think that?"

"Just the way they were dressed."

"You're watching way too many movies." His scowl deepens. "Look, you really don't have to worry about it. From now on, I'll make sure that I never lose sight of you."

He steps back. "Lock the door behind you." He turns to leave.

"Wait," I call out and he pauses, then stares at me over his shoulder.

"Are you going to sleep in your car?"

He arches an eyebrow at me.

"I mean, come one, you already slept on the couch last night—"

"And look where that got us."

I squeeze my fingers together. "I… I'll make sure not to disturb you at night."

He shakes his head, "It's not a good idea, especially after—"

"What happened out there?"

He holds my gaze. "Yes, that's precisely why."

"Would that be so bad?" I whisper.

His gaze intensifies. He searches my features. "Yes," he snaps. "Yes, it would be."

"For you or for me?"

"For both of us." A nerve throbs at his temple.

"I…I don't care anymore."

"But I do." He pivots and begins to walk down the steps, and damn it, I can't let him go. Not yet. I surge forward, grip his arm, and he freezes. He glances down at where my fingers are wrapped around his arm, then he raises his gaze to mine. "Let me go."

"No," I shake my head, "I can't, Baron."

"This is not right." A muscle twitches above his cheekbone.

"Why not?" I swallow. "Edward left me. Likely, he isn't coming back."

"You don't know that."

"Even if he did... I... I don't know if I want to be with him anymore."

"Don't you?" He bends his knees, peers into my eyes. I stare into his bright blue gaze and the intensity of it sweeps through my core. My heart begins to pound and my pulse rate ratchets up. I glance away from him.

"That's what I thought."

He pulls away, stalks back to the car and this time, I let him go.

He walks around, to the driver's side, slides in, and slams the door. The echo reverberates around the empty street, wraps around me, settles inside my empty soul. I turn and walk inside, tears streaming down my cheeks.

I shut the door behind me and my bag slips from my hands. I stumble inside, to the bedroom, switch on the light, then manage to take off my clothes before stepping into the bathroom. I step inside the shower cubicle, start the shower, and the steam from the water envelops me. I sink down in a corner of the cubicle. I wrap my arms around my knees, bend my head and let the tears flow in earnest. Shit, shit, shit. I hug my knees more tightly to my chest, lower my forehead to mash it against my knees, trying to obliterate the pounding in my head. What the hell? Those men. I'm afraid to think of what they could have done to me if Baron hadn't saved me. He rescued me. He's been taking care of me.

But I'm not over Edward. I'm not sure I ever will be. He's my first, and everything is so recent.

But Baron...I need him. I feel safe with him. When his arms are wrapped about me, when he is near me, when his scent enfolds me, it feels like anything is possible. It's as if I've found another part of me. How could something so wrong, feel so right? How can I feel so much for him in such little time? Why does everything with him feel so inevitable?

This is wrong... All wrong... I am, clearly, messed up in my head. I have been from the beginning. It's why I'd never been able to accept that my father could possibly want to be with someone else so soon after my mother's death. And here I am, attracted to two men... At the same time. What am I going to do?

I curl into myself and weep harder. Why did my Mom have to die so early? Would she have understood what I am going through? If I spoke to Raisa about it, I know what she'd say. That I don't need either of them. That's how she is—one-hundred percent devoted to her career. But that isn't me. Dance fills the creative core of me...but since I'd embraced that part of me, it's like the feminism in me had come to the fore. I want more. I want all of it. To be independent, to run my own business, to have a man, to have a family... I want it all. At least, that's what I'd thought. This curve ball that life has leveled at me... I have no idea what to do with it.

If only I could decide, one way or the other... If only I could forget about Edward... But I can't. That much is clear. He'll always be important to me... I'll always love him... And this thing with Baron? What is it, then? Shit, I have no idea. I swallow down the tears that still threaten, then rise to my feet, stumble. The ground rises up to meet me, stops, as I am hauled upright and against a hard chest.

"You came," I whisper.

"I couldn't stay away."

18

Baron

I'd pushed back my seat in the car, tried to settle in for the night, turned this way and that, tried to make myself comfortable. And failed. Those green eyes—tortured, helpless, filled with conflicting emotions that mirrored mine. The way she had met my gaze, and I had seen then what she feels for me... And then, she had looked away. And I had known she still has feelings for Edward.

Damn the man. Why does he always have to be there to turn my life upside down? Why did he have to put me in this situation while he's off doing what he does best—finding himself somewhere? If only the rest of us had that luxury... Some of us...don't even know who we are anymore. My past has been buried and no amount of searching will unearth the boy I had once been. The one before the incident, the one who'd believed he had a future. The one who'd had dreams of becoming a Cricketer, of representing his country on the pitch... I'd gone on to do that alright, just on a different kind of playing field.

One which had helped bring some discipline into my life. Which had grounded me, given me something to focus on so I could move past the tattered remains of my life. In a way, it had helped me to find a part of myself. Except, I never felt fulfilled. Never felt whole…

Not until I met her… She resonates with the deepest parts of me, the parts I've tried to hide deep inside. The parts which now insist there is more to life. Fuck. I can't afford to think that way. Can't afford this crazy attraction that makes me want to take care of her in a completely different manner from what Edward had intended. Or had he?

Is this why he'd pushed us together?

Had he known that we'd be attracted to each other?

Had he wanted me to…fuck his woman? Keep her warm while he's away, and then what? Relinquish her when he comes back? Fuck. I'd sat up then, gotten out of the car. I'd turned toward the house, found it still in darkness, except for a faint glow from the bedroom window…and somehow…somehow… It hadn't felt right. To leave her alone after what had happened. She'd been attacked and I had hauled her back and deposited her without asking her how she was, or if she'd been hurt. If she needed anything. Yeah, I could do that. Just go in and make sure she was okay? I'd walked in—found the door unlocked and sworn aloud. Damn her, couldn't she do this one small thing that I'd asked her to do?

I'd stomped through the living room, the bedroom, and headed toward the sound of the shower of the bathroom. I shouldn't have peeked in, but in my defense, the door was open and I had wanted to make sure she was okay. Honestly, that's all it was. I'd spotted her on the floor of the shower cubicle and my heart had cracked. My legs had moved against my volition and I'd realized I was walking toward her. I'd opened the shower door and caught her as she had stumbled. Had pulled her to me, enfolding her in my embrace.

"I'm sorry…so sorry." I'm not sure what I'm apologizing for, except it feels like I should. "I'm sorry they attacked you." I tuck her head under my chin. "So sorry I didn't reach you earlier."

She clings to me, buries her head against my shirt and cries harder. I sink down and pull her into my lap. She curls into me, hooks her fingers into the lapels of my shirt and continues to sob. My heart stutters. A hot sensation stabs at my chest. I rock her against me, drag my fingers down her hair and hold her close to me.

"Shh," I croon, "it's okay, baby, let it out. I am so sorry I didn't take better care of you. I promise I won't let anyone hurt you."

She turns her face into the 'V' of skin exposed by my shirt. Her shoulders heave as the water pours down on us. I continue to rock her, rub my hand over her back. I wrap my arms around her and hold her until the sobs subside in intensity. She rubs her cheek against my chest, snuggles in further.

"Better?"

She nods.

I reach up to shut off the shower and she stiffens. "Don't leave me."

"I'm not going anywhere." I rise with her in my arms then step out onto the bathmat. "I'm going to make a mess of your space," I mutter.

She only curls up into my chest. I walk over to the counter next to the sink, try to place her on it, but she refuses to let me go.

"I need to dry you."

She shakes her head.

"I need to get out of my wet clothes," I insist.

She peeks up at me from under her eyelashes. "Can I watch?" Her green eyes flare with desire, with hurt.... With something else that I don't dare label yet.

"That...would not be advisable."

"Fuck that," she mumbles.

I bark out a laugh. "You always surprise me, you know that, Eve?"

I try to pull away and she wraps her legs around my waist, that's when I remember she is completely naked. I mean, of course, I'd known that she was naked. It just hadn't completely sunk in... Not until she presses her core into the hard column that tents my pants. "Ava." I wrap my fingers around the back of her neck and apply just enough pressure.

She tilts her chin up, gazes into my eyes. "Fuck me, Baron, please."

"If I do, we'll both regret it."

"If you don't, we'll regret it more."

Fuck. Fuck. Fuck. I wrap her dripping locks around my hand and tug. She gasps and her breathing quickens.

"If I fuck you, there's no going back."

She swallows.

"If I shag you, I won't be able to give you up. Ever."

Her lips kick up. "And I thought men loved to fuck and walk away."

"You knew it was never going to be like that between us."

She scowls. "So, you have fucked and walked away from other women?"

I smirk. "What do you want me to say to that?"

"Nothing." Her gaze narrows. "I'd prefer you to make good on your words, instead."

"If we cross this line," I rake my gaze across her futures, "things will get very complicated."

"They already are." She licks her lips, and the blood drains to my groin.

"If I fuck you, I won't stop at half measures. I won't hold back. I'll take everything you are willing to give me and demand anything you can't. I'll want you to give yourself to me not just physically, but emotionally, mentally. I'll possess you, body and soul. I'll imprint myself in every cell of your body. I'll own you so completely that you won't be able to separate where you begin and where I end. I'll dominate you so completely that you'll not be able to uncouple from me. I'll ask for control of your every emotion, your every thought, your every need. All of it will begin and end with me. Are you willing to take that? Ava? Are you?" I bend down and thrust my face in hers. "Tell me, will you be able to withstand this?"

19

Ava

A shudder runs down my spine. My belly trembles. If I touched myself now, I'd feel the wetness between my legs and it wouldn't be from the shower. The blood thuds at my pulse points. My head spins. The intensity of this man… And his words…? They're filthy and hot and such a freakin' turn on. Lust coils deep in my belly. My thighs clench. I try to close them, but he's standing between my legs so I only end up pushing my melting core into the hard rod that tents his pants.

"Tell me, Ava," he demands, "are you willing to submit to me?"

"I…" I swallow. "Why would I do that?"

"Because you want to?"

"That's not true." I try to pull away, but he doesn't let me.

I tip up my chin, holding his gaze, "I... I am a strong independent woman who—"

"Wants to silence her mind and inspire her body. When you are with me, nothing else will matter because you are all that matters to me. When you are with me, you don't have to think. You don't have to make choices. Well, except for deciding you want to be in this relationship with me."

His lips twist.

"When you are with me, you are exposed but free, because you know that you are safe with me. Even when participating in the most depraved and disgusting acts, and there will be many of those," his grin widens, "yet to me, you will be more beautiful than ever because I can see straight into your soul, your vulnerability, so positively endearing yet so wildly sexy at the same time."

My thighs clench.

"When you are with me, I'll take care of all of your needs. I'll make sure that you never feel alone."

My throat dries. He lowers his head, peers into my face, "When you're with me, I'll treat you with respect and you will obey me, not only because you want to, but because you need to."

His blue eyes lighten to those burning chips of ice that cut through to my very soul.

"When you're with me, I'll fuck you like you are unbreakable, but care for you like you are the most fragile thing I have ever possessed."

The pulse between my legs flares to life. Oh, my god. Those words... I've never heard anything so filthy, so possessive, so hot... Yet so...tender. Can one man mean all those emotions in one sentence?

"You'll submit to me because I need you to. Because I need you more than you can ever need me." The skin around his eyes stretches tight. "You'll submit to me precisely because you are a powerful, independent woman who wants to unearth the deepest, darkest, most sensual parts of her personality. Because you want to know all of yourself. Because you have the courage to admit that under that sweet, strong exterior, you are as depraved as me. And because," he leans in close enough for our eyelashes to tangle, "in this relationship, the power rests with you."

"H... how's that?" I gulp.

"Without your willingness to submit, there is *no* relationship here.

I may be a Dominant, but I'm not dominating you unless you are a willing Submissive. I can tell you to get on your knees, but only you can decide if you will or not." He gaze narrows, "You feel me, Eve?"

I nod.

"Say it then." His gaze lowers to my mouth, "Tell me what I want to hear from you. Say it aloud."

"Yes." I tip up my chin, "Yes. I want to be your Submissive."

His eyes gleam. "Good," he growls, "that's a good girl."

The flesh between my legs swells, throbs, pulsates to a beat that mirrors the nerve that throbs at his temple. My nipples bead, moisture pools in my core. Why did his approval just turn my world upside down? Like I have spent my entire life searching for it?

"Baron?" I whisper, "What will I have to do?"

He peels back his lips and his teeth sparkle. "Everything I ask of you."

"And what would that be?"

"To submit to my every wish, to trust me to do what is best for you. To allow me to play with you, fuck you, bend you over and bury myself inside you." He leans in closer and I have to tilt my head back to meet his gaze. "Your job will be to be on your back, thighs spread wide, to ride my cock and come all over my dick when I tell you to. To suck on my shaft if, and when, I decide you are allowed to. To turn over and loan me your arse if I decide that's where I want to take you."

My cheeks flush, the drumming between my legs seems to grow big, bigger, huge enough to take over my body. Liquid heat seeps through my veins. Sweat beads my palms. Oh, god, I want him to do all of that, and more. I want him to use me as his personal fuck toy, to make me hurt for his pleasure, to take me like I am his. To empty himself inside of me like he belongs to me.

"What would you have me do first?"

His gaze intensifies. "You don't get to ask the questions." His voice lowers to a hush, and I shiver. "Do you understand?"

I nod.

"Good." He pulls away and I lower my legs. He shrugs off his jacket, tosses it aside, then in one smooth move, reaches behind him, and with one arm, pulls off his shirt. OMG, that smooth move, that perfect, gloriously masculine, confident move… I gulp. My throat dries. All the moisture seems to have emptied to the space between my legs. His biceps flex and his chest planes undulate. I take in the expanse of his gorgeous chest, the sculpted eight-pack—yeah, definitely eight-pack—the concave stomach, the trail of hair disappearing down into his waist band. He pulls off his boots and socks, then unzips his pants and peels them off, along with his boxers. His cock springs free. Thick, long, it points up, the head dark and swollen, a vein running up from the bottom to meet the wetness that shimmers at the crown. It's a beautiful cock. As beautiful as Edward's. I swallow. This is wrong. I shouldn't be comparing them, I shouldn't. Why the hell can't I stop thinking of one without the other? Especially when he is standing in front of me, gloriously naked?

Baron rotates his shoulders. He cracks his neck and the sound seems too loud in the space. My nerve endings pop. I take in a breath and my lungs burn. All of the oxygen in the room seems to have been sucked in by this larger-than-life alphahole who looks me up and down.

"Part your legs."

I blink.

"Now."

I instantly widen my thighs. His gaze drops down to my core and his breathing intensifies. His nostrils flare. "Look at you," he murmurs. "Already wet and glistening. You're throbbing for me, aren't you, little girl? Can't wait to have my cock in your pussy. Can't wait for me to impale you, to thrust inside you, and work my shaft in and out of you. To bury myself in you to the hilt and nail you until you can't move for days."

"Oh." A moan bleeds from my lips. My pussy throbs. My stomach clenches. Moisture drools from my core. "Baron, please," I moan. "Please, please, please."

"Hmm." He winds his fingers around his fat dick and pumps himself, once, twice. His shaft increases in length, thickens, swells, and the crown throbs; precum drips from the slit on the head and my mouth waters. My fingertips tingle and I curl my fingers at my side.

"Do you want to touch me?"

I nod.

"Can't wait to take me down your throat, and wrap your tongue around my length and suck me until I come?"

My pussy squeezes in on itself. The emptiness in my core grows bigger, wider, clawing at me, tugging on me, wanting, needing to feel that beautiful dick of his in between my legs.

"Yes." I gasp. "Yes, Baron."

"Not yet."

I blink.

"On your knees, little girl."

"What?"

"Don't ask me to repeat myself."

I slide down from the counter, then sink to my knees.

"Good girl."

I flush. Shit, this is crazy. Why do I like his compliments? Why is it so important that he praise me? My nipples pebble. My breasts seem to swell. My pussy lips are so engorged…too engorged. I need relief. I need to find a way to fill that gaping space in between them. I need… I squeeze my thighs together and he clicks his tongue.

"What?" I scowl.

"No cheating."

"What do you mean?"

"You can't give yourself relief."

"I wasn't."

"No lying, Eve."

I huff. "I wasn't…"

"Yes, you were."

"No."

"Yes."

"Finally, something you're saying yes to."

He chuckles. "Smart and sassy. Gorgeous and full of spirit. Your mouth is as beautiful as your cunt, you know that?"

I swallow. Heat flushes my skin…which feels too tight for my body. My scalp tingles. My toes curl. Every part of me seems to be awakening. Parts of me that I never knew existed seem to be coming alive. My core trembles. My chest hurts. Liquid heat pools in my belly.

"Baron," I whine, "please."

His lips kick up. And that smirk. OMG. So hot, so mean. He reaches for a towel then squats down in front of me. His thigh muscles bunch, his chest planes flex, and his biceps make that little twitch that nearly drives me insane. I swallow, watch as he drags the towel about my shoulders, down my chest, across my breasts, my stomach, my thighs, in between my legs. I shudder. And for all that, his touch is impersonal, almost clinical, as he dries me. He tosses the towel aside, then grabs another and drops it over my shoulders. "Stay." He rises to his feet, and damn him, but that means I am at eye level with his glorious, fat peen. Argh. My mouth waters. My lips part. I reach forward and he steps back. *What the—?* I tip up my chin, and he waggles a finger at me. "Not yet, Eve."

"But I wanna..." *Did I just whine? I whined. What the hell is he doing to me?* I am a strong independent woman, ready to forge ahead to make a mark on the world on my terms. This...mewling, writhing creature, who'd do anything for her master... Her lover? This isn't me. And hold on, why am I thinking of him as my master? Or my lover, for that matter? Considering we haven't even slept together. Okay, so he'd made me come. Hard. More than once. And now he's standing in all his naked glory in front of me, smirking down at me, with a twist of those gorgeous, kissable, pouty lips that I want to bite down on.

His grin widens. His eyes twinkle. Of course, he knows exactly how turned on I am just now. *Jerk.*

"You wanna come, little Eve?" He places his palm against my cheek. "Do you?"

"You know I do."

He nods, "Pass your first test, and we'll see."

Wait... What?

Turning, he stalks out.

The bastard heads out of the bathroom, leaving me there on my knees. Naked. At least, I am not cold because he'd wrapped the towel around me. Still... *Asshole.* I stay where he's left me. My knees begin to hurt. My thighs spasm. A bead of sweat slides down my back and I shake off my towel. Thanks to the earlier hot shower, I am warm and the remnants of the heat seems to cling to the very air that I breathe in. My left shoulder blade itches. I reach back to scratch myself, lose my balance and fall over. Gah. This is stupid. Like really stupid. How dare he simply leave me when I am horny? Shit, I've been horny since... Meeting Edward. And his fucking me had only whetted my appetite.

Then, Baron comes along and my needs seem to have escalated to a whole new height. I feel hungry and torn apart inside, and so damn lonely. The physical need to be with him crawls across my skin, lodges in my belly. I rise to my feet, march out, through the bedroom, and the living room. I head for the kitchen, enter, then stop. Baron stands with his back to me. His very naked back. His tight glutes are a work of art. Honed and taut, with the hollows at the sides that you'd expect to find on a ballet dancer. They only serve to highlight just how in a shape he is. Does he, like, spend his every, single, free moment working out? And those thick thighs. Jesus, his thighs deserve a sculpture all their own. Right after his dick, that is. I could spend all of my days and nights worshipping at the altar of his cock. Argh. I did not just think that. I head into the room. He swings around, rakes his gaze up and down my body.

"I was expecting you."

20

———————

Baron

"You…you were?" Her chin wobbles.

I'd wondered how long she'd last there. It had been a test for her as much as for myself. Though why I am stringing her along so… when all it does is heighten my need for her...is anyone's guess. Maybe because I am a masochist?

I smirk and she frowns.

I take a step forward. She freezes. I fold my arms across my chest, jerk my chin to the ground in front of me.

"No way," she grouses. "I am not kneeling, again."

"I'm not asking."

She presses her lips together, then stomps across to me. Her tits jiggle and her thighs shake. My shaft lengthens further, if that were possible. She lowers herself to her knees, folds her arms in front of her.

"Good."

I grab a chair, plant it in front of her. Then pick up the bowl of soup. I sit down on the chair, scoop up the soup and hold it out. "Eat."

She frowns.

"You cooked?"

"If you call opening a can of soup that, then yes."

She darts me a quick glance from under her eyelashes. "Do I detect a tinge of judgement?" She huffs.

"You need to eat better."

"I eat plenty, thank you very much."

"It's not the quantity but the quality that I'm questioning."

"I hate cooking," she mumbles.

"And I like cooking for you."

"Oh." She opens her mouth, and I slide the spoon between her lips. "Eat first. You are going to need your energy."

She swallows, stares at me. "For what?"

"What do you think?"

Her cheeks tinge. She parts her lips and the sight of her wet plump lips? Bloody hell. This was a bad idea. I should have taken her earlier. But that...would not have been right. Not when she still hadn't recovered from her earlier run-in with those men. I tighten my fingers around the spoon, which jerks. I dip it back in the bowl, continue to feed her.

She takes a few more mouthfuls, then jerks her chin in my direction. "You're not eating."

"I will…soon."

"The soup's almost finished."

"That's not my dinner."

"Eh?" She frowns, opens her mouth to receive the next spoonful. My cock thickens and my balls tighten. I dip the spoon into the bowl, offer the last of the soup to her. She swallows it, then asks, "Then what will you be eating?"

"What do you think?" I place the bowl on the floor, then straighten.

"You don't mean…" Her face grows redder. "You mean —"

I nod.

"On your back, little Eve."

She sits back on her haunches, then lowers herself onto the floor, her knees bent.

"Part your legs."

She spreads wide and I take in the flush that envelops her chest, the pointed nipples, the curves of her breasts, the delectable plumpness of her belly, below that her tender flesh. Her pussy lips are slightly parted and the shy bud of her clit peers out from under the hood. I slide my foot between her thighs, nudge her slit with my big toe. She shivers, tries to close her legs around the intrusion and I click my tongue. "Remember, you don't get to get yourself off."

"Why not?" she whines. "It's not fair."

"Life's not fair, baby." I rub my big toe up her pussy. "Deal with it."

Her entire body jerks. She lifts her pelvis up, tries to ride my toe. I pull back and her breath hitches. "Bastard," she grumbles.

"Technically, not true. My parents may not be happy with my choices in life so far, but they were married when I was born."

"They didn't like you joining the army?"

"To say the least." I press my entire foot against the warmth of her core and she freezes. I push into her center and she moans.

"S-so," she stutters, "did they know that you were imprisoned?"

"I assume the army informed them."

"And that you were freed?"

"I am sure they know of it."

"Do they know that you're back?"

"You really want to do this now?" I snap. "You want to talk about my family right when I am about to get you off?"

"Y...yes." She swallows.

I withdraw my foot, and she thrusts her pelvis forward, chasing the sensations with her pelvis. Good.

I rake my gaze across her features. "What I do or don't do with respect to my family is not your concern."

"But you are." She scowls. "I mean," she looks to the side, then back at me, "it's just human courtesy, you know. They are your family, surely they must worry about you."

"Trust me, they don't. My mother's too busy with her fundraisers and keeping up appearances. And by the time my father is done taking care of his business, and his various mistresses in different parts of the world, he has no time left for me."

I drag my big toe up her wet melting cunt and she shudders. I swipe it down to her opening, and she writhes under me.

Her tits rise and fall, her breath comes in little gasps, color smears her chest, her cheeks, and her lips are parted as she peers up at me from under heavy eyelids. She's magnificent, and fuck I'll never forget this sight of her ready and open and needy on the floor in front of me.

"What always confused me," I continue in a normal tone, "was that I was an only child and his heir, so you'd think he'd be more worried about me, at least, from the point of view of me inheriting his business, and being the bearer of his legacy. But apparently, that makes no difference to him." I raise a shoulder. "As soon as I turned twenty-one, I accessed the trust fund that my grandfather left me. Then, I left home, never looked back. So, you see, Eve, nope, they don't really care about me. "

I had spent the best part of my teens trying to cope with the aftermath of the incident. And then, there had been Edward. Yeah... another mistake of epic proportions that had been...just like the one I am about to make now. And just like the last time, I am helpless. Unable to stop myself. A starving man who's spotted the first glimmer of an oasis in the desert. And what if that turns out to be a mirage? I stare into the face of the woman who's elicited these feelings inside of me. The woman I had sworn to protect. But who is going to protect her from me?

I pull back my foot, then jerk my chin, "Get up."

"What?" She blinks up at me.

"Up." I straighten. "On your feet."

She scowls back, then rises up.

"Come closer."

She huffs. "Lie down, spread your legs. On your feet... Make up your mind assho—"

I grab her hips, yank her close. She squeaks. I lift her up so she's straddled across my lap. "You want me to fuck you?"

She swallows.

"Do you?"

"Y…yes."

"Good." I reach for the condom I'd placed on the table behind me.

"Ah, Baron?"

I turn to her.

"I am on birth control."

"You are?"

"The only person I was with was Edward and he, uh, he'd been celibate for a long time before he was with me."

I stare at her flushed cheeks. Her thick auburn hair in a halo about her shoulders. I am not jealous that Edward took her virginity. I am not upset that he was with her before me. Who the hell am I kidding? A growl rips out of me. "I am clean too," I hold her gaze, "and I am going to wipe every trace of him from your body."

"Baron," she scolds, "it's not a competition."

"Isn't it?" I grab my dick, and fit it to her opening, thrust up, and in one smooth move, I impale her. She screams, griping my shoulders.

"Omigod, omigod," she chants. "You're too big for me."

"You're so small, Eve," I growl.

She wriggles her hips and I squeeze down to hold her in place. "Wait." I grit my teeth. The heat of her, the warmth, the wetness, the way her pussy welcomes me, clamps down on my shaft, clings to my swollen flesh, as she digs her fingernails into my shoulders and groans.

"Baron, it's too much."

"Not enough," I snap. "Nothing is going to be enough after this."

I bring my hand to her breast and squeeze. A moan bleeds from her lips. The sound coils in my chest, slides down to settle in my belly. My cock throbs, aches with the need to possess her completely. "Goddam you," I snarl. "I wanted to go slow, to make you wait, to hold on until I was sure you were ready, but when I am near you, I lose all sense of control."

"You…you do?" She gasps.

"You're inside me, Eve. You drive me crazy, you know that?"

She brings her hands up to frame my face. Her touch is so soft, so soothing. So very different from anything I've faced in the last few years. So sweet. So everything. A ball of emotion clogs my throat. I swallow it down. Focus on the curvy, little woman who's wrapped around my dick. She brings her thumb to my mouth, and I close my lips around the digit. I suck on it and her chest heaves. Her pussy clenches around my dick. I can't stop the growl that rumbles from me. "I need to be deeper in you."

I pump my hips upward, thrust my shaft into her. Her head falls back and her lips part. She snaps her shoulders back and grips her knees on either side of my thighs.

"Like that," I groan. "Just like that."

I begin to nail her, up and down, up and into her. Inside her. Trying to mark every millimeter of her hot, melting channel. She moans, digs her fingernails deeper into my shoulders, thrusts out her breasts in my face. I bend, close my mouth around a nipple and bite. She cries out. "Oh, Baron, please, please, please, I want to come, I need to come. Please."

"Not yet." I lick her swollen flesh, transfer my attention to her other breast. When I suck on her nipple this time, she groans, then pushes her breast further into my mouth. I curl my lips round the distended flesh, sucking on it, digging my teeth into the curve of her tit and she cries out. She tilts her hips, pushing down on me, trying to ride me, and find a rhythm that will get me closer, deeper, much deeper inside her. "Fuck this."

I rise, and with my dick still in her, walk over to the dining room table. I shove the plates and the cutlery aside—yeah, I had actually set the table… Imagine that. What had I been thinking? That I could get us to eat a civilized dinner? I should have known better. Known that as soon as I touched her, things would get out of control. F-u-c-k. I lower her to the table, then hook my arms under her knees and wrap her legs over my shoulders.

She reaches for me and I shake my head. I twist her wrists together, shove them over her head, and wrap her fingers around the edge of the table.

She gazes up at me, pupils blown, the darkness of her irises bleeding out until only a circle of green remains around the circumference.

"Hold on," I order.

"Wh…what?"

"I am going to fuck you now."

21

Ava

Fuck me, now? What the hell? What has he been doing so far? He pulls back then thrusts forward. I am so wet that he slides in to the hilt in one smooth move.

The breath whooshes out of me. His length throbs inside of me, filling me, stretching me to the brim. He seems impossibly big, too thick to have forced his way into my tiny channel. A moan bleeds from my lips. His gaze darts to my mouth. He leans down, rubs his thumb across my lips. "Open," he rasps.

I part my lips and he slides his finger inside. I lick his digit, absorb the salty, testosterone-filled taste of his skin. He slides his other hand under me, inserts his digit inside my pucker and goose-bumps pop on my skin. *Shit, shit, shit. What's he doing to me?* With every hole in my body occupied by him, he begins to fuck me in earnest.

He pulls back, until his cock is poised at the entrance to my channel, then he thrusts forward with such force that the entire table creaks. He propels his hips, rams into me again. My body jerks; the table groans. Heat radiates from the point of contact as he locks his gaze on mine. I can't look away from his hard features — the blue eyes glowing as if lit from within; those massive shoulders of his that roll and flex with each push forward; the bead of sweat that trickles down his cheek. A vein throbs at his temple, the very air around him saturated with the fierceness of his desire. I can't take my eyes off of him. He pulls out, then pistons his hips forward and sinks into me until he bottoms out against my pelvic floor. His balls slap against my arse; the angle pushes the hardness of his dick into the sensitive lower skin of my slit and tendrils of heat flare out from the contact.

He curves his finger inside my back hole, as he pulls his thumb from my mouth, only to replace it with his tongue. He kisses me, sucks on my tongue like he's trying to absorb my very essence into his blood, and that's when the climax sweeps out from my lower belly. It screams up as he releases my mouth, only to command, "Come for me, come all over my dick, sweet Eve."

I shatter. The orgasm crashes over me. Sparks of brightness overwhelm my vision. When it clears, I blink, watch him watching me with an expression I cannot fathom.

He reaches down, brushes his lips over mine, as he begins to pump into me, once-twice-thrice before his features contort. He holds my gaze as he empties himself inside of me with a groan, and oh, my god, that is the hottest sight I have ever seen.

He pulls his thumb out from my back hole, leans over me as he rests his weight on his elbows on either side of me. That's when the table creaks, sways, then collapses. I scream as the world tilts. The next moment, I am on his chest. "What the—?" I blink. "How did you move that quickly?"

"Training," he mutters.

I glance at him, then at the remnants of my poor dining table, then back at his face. A chuckle bubbles up. His lips curve.

"OMG," I snort, "I can't believe we broke the dining table."

"Guess my weight was too much for it?" he suggests.

"It's never seen so much action as in the last fifteen minutes."

"At least, now you don't have to disinfect it," he offers, and that only makes me laugh harder.

"This…this gives an entire new meaning to nailing the table," I sputter.

"You know what you should do after you have sex on a dining table right?"

"What…?" I wipe my tears. "What?"

"Table spoon," he declares.

I stare, then burst out laughing. I laugh until tears roll down my cheeks. Glance up to find him staring at me.

"What?" I blink, "What is it?"

"Nothing." He swallows.

"Are you sure? You seem pale."

"It's," he shakes his head, "it's just when you laughed…" He peers into my face. "It reminded me of…"

"What?"

His gaze intensifies. He glances to the side then back at me, "Seriously, babe, it's nothing."

"Hmm," I pout, "you're hiding something from me."

"And here I was sure you'd tell me off for my poor joke."

"That it was." I nod, "And by the way, you're trying to change the topic."

"Am I that obvious?" He winces, "Clearly, I am losing my touch. That's what happens when I try to have a conversation on an empty stomach."

I stare at him with suspicion.

"What do you mean?"

"I mean," he pulls out of me, then sits up and rises to his feet, taking me with him. He sets my feet on the floor, then continues, "I still haven't eaten. You ready to serve me my dinner?" He waggles his eyebrows.

I glance around the kitchen then back at him. "There's, uh, some leftover pizza in the fridge."

"That's not what I am talking about."

He takes a step forward. I circle the mess of the collapsed dining table, not to mention the dishes he'd shoved to the floor earlier. I am going to have to do without them, considering I don't have the money to replace them. I glance up to find he's moved closer. I skitter back, and he points a finger at me, "Don't move."

"Oh, no, you're not going to command me to stay, just so you can catch me."

"It's not that." He glances around at the floor around my feet.

"Then what is it."

"Just hold it." He puts up a hand. I raise my leg to take a step to the side. He leaps forward, across the broken table, drops to his knees and grabs my ankle before I can place it on the floor. "Hey!" I lose my balance, grab at his head, dig my fingers into his hair to right myself. "What's wrong with you?"

"You were going to step on a piece of crockery." He holds up a shard that must have broken off from one of the plates.

"Oh, no."

"Oh, yes." He smirks, tosses the shard onto the pile of broken furniture that had once been my dining table. Then he stands, scoops me up and tosses me over his shoulder.

"What the—?" I squeak. He turns, steps over the fragments of broken dishes and wooden splinters, and stopping only to switch off the light, heads out of the kitchen.

"Where are you taking me?" I ask, and darn it, my voice sounds breathless… And it's not because I'm turned on. Yea, right, because let's face it, being hauled over his shoulder like I weigh nothing… Okay, it's fucking sexy, and hot. My stomach flip-flops; I squeeze my thighs together to stop the itch that's gnawing at my core. Bloody hell, he just fucked me and now I want him to go again. Gah!! *Shut up, slut, what the hell is wrong with you?*

He veers into the bedroom, stalks over to the bed and throws me down. I bounce once on my back, my hair flowing around my face. I shake back the strands, stare up to find him looming over me; a wicked smirk curls his lips.

"No, no, no," I mutter as I crawl back on the bed. The light from the half-open door of the bathroom streams in. His silhouette is massive, a dark, solid figure that eats up all the light. He reaches the edge of the bed, plants his hands on his hips. "We have a problem," he rumbles.

"Do we?"

He nods. "I still haven't had dessert."

"D…dessert?" I squeak.

His grin widens. "The best kind, babe, where I get to eat all of it."

My core clenches, liquid heat crawls between my legs, and I squeeze my thighs together. "Th…that sounds nice."

He chuckles, "Oh, you have no idea, baby."

He places a knee on the bed. I push away from him. He swoops down, grabs my ankle, and I yell. Turn on my hands and knees, try to crawl away. He simply hauls me back, until my feet touch the edge of the bed. My heart beat ratchets up; my pulse pounds at my temples. He grabs my other ankle and I yell. Flail out with my legs, or try to, because he has a grip on me, and he's stronger than me. So he's, pretty much, restraining me, and I don't want to escape, not really. But damn, if I'm going to allow him to conquer me so quickly. Adrenaline laces my blood. I kick out with my leg, and must take him by surprise, because his grip loosens. I scream, lunge forward, throwing all of my weight into it. Only, he grabs my free ankle and hauls me back again. A giggle breaks free, then another. Damn it, I am getting hysterical. My pulse rate speeds up. My heart hammers so fast, I am sure it's going to break out of my chest. And my eyes start to burn. "Let me go, you oaf!" I howl.

He releases his hold on my legs instantly, and I pause. *What the —? Did he unhand me? He did set me free. He did—* I move forward, but he's already on me. He lowers his body over mine, pins me down with his hips. The warmth of him enfolds me; his strength cocoons me; his big body is all around me. "Shh!" He curls his fingers about my nape, "Shh, baby, no need to panic. I'll take care of you."

The hold on my neck is erotic and comforting at the same time. My breasts swell and my nipples harden. I stay frozen until he begins to massage my neck.

"Ah…" A sigh escapes me as he digs his thumb into a knot right at the point of where my neck meets my shoulder.

"Easy, darlin'," he croons, like I am a skittish horse or a rabbit about to dart away. He applies enough pressure that I lower my cheek into the mattress. "Relax," he drawls, as he continues to dig his magic fingers down the length of my neck, into my shoulder. I sense him move, and glance sideways to find he's straddling me. His thick thighs bunch as he leans forward, and wraps his warm palms about my shoulders. He digs his fingers into my muscles, into the knots, and with circular movements soothes them away.

"That's sooo good." My shoulders relax and my muscles unwind. A delicious warmth grips me. I close my eyes as he continues to tend to me. He pushes my hair off my neck, I feel a slight touch and crack open one eye. "Did you just kiss me on my neck?" I ask

"What do you think?" I hear the laughter in his voice and can't stop my lips from curving in response.

"I think you're too macho for just tender gestures."

"You'd be right." He slides his fingers against my scalp, and my entire body hums. Who knew I had an erogenous zone there?

"Mmmm," I glance up at him from under heavy eyelashes, "this is wayyy too relaxing."

"Good." He continues to massage my neck, my shoulders, down my shoulder blades, my hips. By the time he reaches my butt, I am so far gone, I don't even react as he squeezes each butt cheek. My pussy hums, my thigh muscles respond, the rest of me is way too at ease. I sense him move again, as he slides down, feel the heat of his body, as he crouches over me. Then a wetness invades my most forbidden place. I squeak, angle my head and see him lick me from my slit up the valley between my arse cheeks.

"Omigod." Heat flushes my cheeks. "What…what are you doing?"

"Shh, don't tense up now." He reaches up to slide his hand under my breast. He cups it, then pinches my nipple. My pussy instantly clenches, as does my arsehole. He makes a guttural sound deep in his throat as I moan.

"Baron, please," I gasp, "I am not ready yet."

He simply releases his hold on my breast, only to shove three fingers into my melting core. He begins to work me there and moisture pools between my legs. "Good girl," he croons, his breath hot against my hip. He drags my cum up my seam and smears it across my pucker.

I tense and he massages my hip. "Relax," he orders.

"Are you… are you…?"

"Going to take your arse?"

He pulls out of my pussy only to squeeze my arsecheeks and pry them apart. I whip around in time to see him spit on my arsehole.

22

———

Baron

"Did you just do what I think you did?" Her voice wavers.

I glance up at her, "What do you think I did?" I hold her gaze as I rub my spit into her back opening.

"Did you just…spit…there?" Her face reddens further. So fucking cute. This girl is so naive. How the hell did I get involved with her? More to the point, how had she gotten entangled with first Edward and then me? Even more worrying, why the hell am I developing feelings for her? I am, no question. It's why I've tried to walk away from her so many times, and failed. It's why I lean over and press a kiss to her pouting mouth.

I swipe my tongue across her mouth, then deepen the kiss. I bite down on her lips and she gasps. I ease my tongue inside, while I slide one finger inside her back hole. Her body shudders. I cup her pussy, press down on her clit. She moans and I work my finger past the circle of her sphincter.

I lean back, watch her features closely as I saw my finger in and out of her. I add a second finger and she swallows. Her eyelids shutter down.

"Look at me, babe."

She cracks open her eyes, and I hold her gaze as I scissor my fingers inside of her.

"Baron." Her shoulders shudder. I slide three fingers of my other hand inside her pussy, then proceed to fuck her with my digits. In and out, in and out. Her pussy clamps down on my fingers; her mouth opens in surprise. I sense the orgasm sweep up her body, her features tense in that way which indicates she's close, so close.

"Baron, I need to… I have to…"

"Come," I command. And her eyes roll back in her head. A cry tumbles from her lips and she arches back, then collapses. Moisture gushes out from her core and I scoop up her juices. I pull my fingers out of her backhole, before I smear her juices at the entrance. Then I position my dick against her puckered opening.

She moans and her eyelids flutter open. "Did I come again?" She blinks.

"And you will many more times before the night is out." I ease the crown of my shaft into her tight opening. She tenses and I bend and kiss her cheek, the shell of her ear. I bite down on her earlobe and she shudders. I slip inside her a little more. The heat, the tightness... If her pussy is heaven, surely this is…as close to hell as it gets. A hell where pain and pleasure weave around each other like the coils of Satan's snake in darkness.

"Baron?" She frowns at me. "Are you okay?"

I shake my head. "I should be asking you that."

"It's just for a second there, you seemed to —"

"Black out?"

She nods.

"It's just…" I glance down at where my dick disappears inside her arse and my balls tighten. "You, Eve. It's you. Your body, your voice, your scent, your seductive holes that I can't keep out of."

She folds her arms under her cheek, watches me with those large green eyes. And something inside me, knotted for so long, seems to dissolve. Break. Disappear like it never existed. But that's a lie. I am marked, tainted by my past. She still has her future ahead of her. And here I am…taking everything she's offering, snatching up what she doesn't, demanding that she give herself to me. For what? So I can stain her with the same brush that painted me? So my mistakes will taint her?

I grip her arse cheeks, pry them apart. "Let me in, Eve."

She swallows and her breathing speeds up.

"I won't stop until I have taken you, marked you everywhere he has."

She bites down on her lower lip and my cock twitches. I tilt my hips, push forward, sink in another millimeter. She thrusts her hips back, and I push past the tight ring of her sphincter. A groan bleeds from her lips. My belly clenches. Heat grips me and sweat slides down my back. I release her butt, only to grab her hips and pull. "Up, on your hands and knees," I snap.

She pushes up as I pump forward, and sink inside her channel. A growl rips from me. I lean over her, press a kiss to her shoulder. "You okay, babe?"

She shudders.

"Tell me you're okay, Eve, that you want me to continue."

She hunches her shoulders.

"Eve?"

She nods.

"Say that you want me to continue."

"I…" she gulps, "I want you to fuck my arse."

Thank fuck.

I lean over, kiss the side of her neck. Bring my arm around her waist as I press my mouth to her shoulder, the damp skin between her shoulder blades. "You're fucking gorgeous, you know that? You're the kind of woman I never thought I'd meet."

"You don't have to be nice to me." She chuckles. "You're already in my arse."

I laugh. "That mouth of yours." I reach up and nuzzle her hair. "I fucking love it."

"And I love…" She gasps. "Uh, I think I am falling for you."

"Wait, what did you say?" I pause. "Repeat yourself."

"It was nothing." She turns her head in my direction. "Honestly, just a slip of the tongue."

I frown. "It didn't seem that way, from where I am."

"No, Baron, really, it's just... You know..." She raises a shoulder. "Just ignore me."

I glare at her. "Don't you dare develop feelings for me, Eve."

She half smiles. "What would you do if I did?"

"I'll..." I begin to withdraw and she reaches down between us and grabs my balls. She squeezes and my thigh muscles spasm. "Fuck."

"Exactly." She massages me, tugs on my balls. She handles them like they belong to her... Like I belong to her... *Fuck... No, no, no.* What the hell am I thinking? This can't happen. She can't fall for me...and I... Fuck me... I am already half-way in love with her. I knew I was developing feelings for her, but love? Fucking love. What is that about?

She tugs on my balls, drags her hands up to where my dick is still embedded inside her. She circles her hips, begins to move, and heat races out from the point of contact. I wrap my fingers about her hips, pull out, then thrust in. She releases me, plants her hands on the bed, and thrusts out her butt. This woman... She's going to kill me with her openness, her willingness, her surrender to me... How she accepts me into her body, her heart... How she can bare her soul and share her deepest feelings. If only I could be half as open as that... Perhaps, we could have a future. And when she had laughed earlier... I could have sworn she was the same woman I'd seen on the railway platform not too long ago.

And yet, I can't share my past with her. Can't give her everything she deserves. Not when my secrets hold me back. Not when everything inside me tells me I need to find a way out before things get more complicated. Just for one night though, I can hold her, cherish her, fuck her like she is mine, love her like she is the only one for me.

And then when you leave her? What's she going to do then? Are you going to break her heart like that asshole Edward did?

But she loves Ed. She doesn't feel anything close enough for me. She did say that she thinks she's falling for me. After almost saying she loves me... which is precisely why I need to leave in the morning, before things become more complicated.

I pull out, then slide inside her, slowly, slowly, every millimeter of my shaft dragging against her channel. Her body trembles. Her hips twitch. I retreat, until I am poised at the edge of her opening, then thrust forward. Her body bucks. The bed creaks. I impale her, bury myself in her tightness and she cries out. Heat flushes my skin, tendrils of sensations pour out from where we are joined. "Fuck, Eve, F-u-c-k." I begin to move in earnest.

She throws her head back, pushes back, meets my every thrust. "Omigod, Baron, I'm coming, I'm going to—"

"Come with me, Eve," I growl. "Come right now."

She cries out again and her body shudders. Her shoulders snap back before she curves her body, screaming as she collapses.

I wrap one arm about her waist, holding her up as I pump into her, again and again. The tension at the base of my spine coils tightly, twists in on itself as I cram myself inside her one last time. My balls draw up, the vibrations flare out from my groin, up my back, to my extremities, and I empty myself inside of her.

23

Ava

I come awake to the sensation of something hot and wet lapping at my cunt. I part my legs, tilt my hips to allow better access. He eases his tongue inside my aching pussy, saws it in and out of me. A warmth trembles out from the point of contact. Heat suffuses my skin. I moan and arch my back, pushing out my breasts. My nipples pebble, becoming throbbing points of pain. I bring my hands up and squeeze them. A shudder runs down my spine. My belly flutters as he increases the pace of his ministrations. He drags his hands up my inner thighs, urging me to spread my legs wider, then uses his fingers to pull my pussy lips apart as he swipes his tongue around my swollen clit. A groan bleeds from my lips. My toes curl. He continues to swirl his tongue across my melting core, then thrusts it back inside my channel. He plunges that sinful tongue in and out of me, in and out, until shudders grip me. He releases my pussy lips, only to grind the heel of his hand into my clit, even as he slides a hand around and eases a finger inside my back hole. I moan again, release my breasts and bury my fingers in his thick hair. I tug on the strands and a growl rumbles up his massive chest. The vibrations shudder across my core, and that only turns me on even more. The climax ripples up from my toes, up my thighs, eddies in my core, before it slides up my spine. I arch my back, throw my head back and moan as the orgasm grips me. My core clenches and moisture slides down from between my legs. He continues to eat me out, slurping at me like I am the most delicious fruit ever. He licks me clean, then moves up to fit his lips to mine. He kisses me and I taste myself and him—that edgy danger that is so very Baron. He moves onto his back, pulls me onto him, then kisses the top of my head. "Sleep, little Eve."

His voice soothes me and I burrow into him, and let the darkness overwhelm me.

When I wake next, I am tucked into his side.

He's sprawled out, taking up most of the bed, his arm flung out, with my head pillowed on it. I rake my gaze across his chest, down to where the sheets are pooled around his waist…and tented…at his crotch. Oh! O-k-a-y, doesn't this guy ever sleep? Is it morning wood? Must be, right? I glance up and my gaze clashes with his brilliant blue eyes. I swallow, watch him watch me. His hair is ruffled, thanks to how I'd pulled on it, no doubt. His jaw is shadowed and he looks rumpled, more relaxed than I've ever seen him, and yet, also alert. He's always alert, my Baron.

What? Why did I call him *my* Baron? He's not my…anything. My lover? Maybe… Nothing else. Except… Shit. I'd almost blurted out that I love him, then tried to cover it by saying I think I'm falling for him. How lame is that? And he…hadn't responded in kind. Of course, not. Why would he? I am simply a job for him… Albeit, one from whom he can also draw out orgasms… Not that I am complaining about that… But why the hell did I have to fall for him? More to the point, why tell him? Clearly, the sex is addling my brain. That's the only reason I hadn't been able to shut up. And he… Well?

Clearly, he has no such issues. He looks w-a-y too awake, like he had a good sleep and is ready to face the world. Like a night of mind-blowing sex is normal for him. Like he hadn't just brought me to orgasm so many times that I could still feel the imprint of his dick and his tongue in between my legs. Hmm. Wonder if I can't return the favor? I mean, fair's fair. Right? Without taking my gaze off of him, I slide my hand under the sheet. When I close my fingers about his already erect cock, his nostrils flare.

Oh, good. He's not as impervious as he'd like me to think. I grip his shaft, and my fingers barely meet around the circumference. Shit, is this guy huge or what? I massage him from base to crown and I swear his cock swells further. His gaze narrows. His shoulders tense. He doesn't move though. Simply holds my gaze with those intense blue eyes of his as I squeeze his shaft and knead his length over and over again. His jaw hardens. A pulse leaps to life at his temple. And a shiver runs down my spine. I slide down until I'm settled between his legs, still under the cover. I lower my head toward his cock and his chest planes flex. I bring my fingers to his base, hold him upright, then tip my chin down and run my tongue across the head. A growl rumbles up his chest, and my core clenches at his response. With this man…

Everything he says and does seems to be calculated to arouse me, and damn him, he's not even trying. He just has to be in the same space for his pheromones to saturate the air, and I'd be turned on. Moisture pools between my legs as I dip my head and close my mouth around the swollen crown. His eyelids flutter down. He glares at me from under those thick eyelashes…which only emphasize how masculine the rest of him is. I swirl my tongue around the circumference of the head and his belly muscles jump. I bring my other hand down, cup his balls and squeeze, and a groan rips from him. His biceps tense, his shoulders stiffen. His features grow harder, and damn, if this isn't the most erotic sight I have ever seen. I may be sucking his dick, but I have him by his balls. Adrenaline laces my blood. A feeling of power grips me. I massage his balls, tilt my head and take him down my throat.

Instantly, my gag reflex kicks in. I cough. Tears well up, spit drools from my mouth and I pull back, only he clamps his hand on the back of my head and holds me in place.

"You'd better finish what you started, Eve."

Oh. His hard voice chafes across my skin. My nerve endings pop. Every part of me seems to flare to life. To challenge him. To please him. I stare at him, forcing my neck muscles to relax, to breathe through my nose, as I stay poised with his dick on the edge of my mouth. I lick him again, drag my tongue across the sensitive skin of the crown and his lips twist.

"That the best you can do?" he rumbles, and my belly flip-flops. *I'll show you what I can do, you jerk.* I dip my chin, and slide him inside my mouth. I close my lips around him, drag my teeth across the silky skin and his smirk vanishes. I breathe through my nose as I take him down my throat, and a growl rips from him. His fingers dig into my hair and he tugs. Goosebumps flare across my skin. I begin to suck him in earnest, pull back, then slide him inside my mouth...and again. I swallow and his chest rises and falls. "Fuck, Eve. Fuck." He tugs on my hair, so I pull back, then pushes me down. His gaze transfixed on my lips.

"The sight of my dick disappearing in your mouth, woman," he growls, "I'll never forget it as long as I live."

He begins to fuck my mouth in earnest, maneuvering me into just the right position that gives him the most satisfaction. Throughout, I continue to massage his balls, squeezing, tugging, watching as his body responds. As his thigh muscles clench, as his belly tightens, as color smears his cheeks.

His shaft thickens, broadens, fills my mouth, stretches my jaws. Pain slides down my neck; tears flow from my eyes. Still, I don't protest. Still, his gaze holds mine. The skin around his eyes stretches. He increases the pace, pulls me back, then forward, until all I can see is him, taste the salty-dark essence of him, smell his edgy, masculine, mountain breeze scent, now tinged with something more lush... Tinged with me. His balls draw up and my core clenches; my toes curl. Spit drips from my mouth and he shudders. "Fuck, I'm coming, Eve. I'm going to come in your mouth and you'd better swallow every last drop, you feel me?"

His hips jerk and he flings out his other arm, grabs the sheet, as his hold on my hair tightens. He growls as he shoots his cum down my throat. The hot liquid fills my mouth, spills over, and he reaches down and scoops up the overflow. He pulls out of me, uses his dick to smear his cum across my lips, then yanks me up and fixes his mouth to mine.

24

Baron

The taste of me on her lips… It's potent and erotic and so bloody right. I turn until she's once more on her back, under me, where she belongs. *My woman. Mine.* I soften the kiss, lick her lips, swipe my tongue across the seam of her mouth. She moans at the back of her throat, and the sound goes straight to my head. My heart stutters and something hot fills my chest. I tear my mouth from hers, peer into her face. "What the fuck are you doing to me?" I mutter.

"The same thing you're doing to me." Her features are serious, her gaze slightly clouded. Her pupils still dilated from the blow job she gave me.

I cup her cheek, drag my thumb across her lips. "That…" I swallow, "that was incredible."

Her mouth curves, her eyes sparkle up at me, and something shifts again in my chest. *Shit, this isn't good.* This can't happen. I can't let myself get close—okay, closer—to her. Considering I already have feelings for her.

I pull back, then swing my legs over the side of the bed and stand up. "Don't you have a class to teach?"

"I do," she replies, "but uh... I thought I could cancel?"

"Don't." Shit, that...didn't come out right. I turn around to find her staring at me, a hurt look in her eyes, and my heart, my stupid heart breaks. Bloody hell, since when have I become so tuned into her? I sit down on the edge of the bed and pull her close. "Hey, hey, come on." I rub her back. "I only meant, don't change your plans for me."

"Don't do that," she snarls. "Seriously, Baron, don't pull away from me."

"I..." I rake my gaze across her features, "I'm not."

"You are."

"It's your imagination."

"Oh, please." She tosses her hair over her shoulder, "You jump out of bed like you can't bear to be with me a minute more, when—"

"The truth is exactly the opposite."

She frowns. "What do you mean?"

I release her, then stand up again... Only to put distance between us, because if I continue to hold her in my arms, there's no way I'll be able to focus long enough to get my thoughts together. And right now, that's important. I need to get my shit together long enough to establish boundaries. It's the only way I can get through this—whatever this is between us—intact.

"I am way too attracted to you. I am developing feelings for you, Eve, and that's a problem."

"You don't say?" she mutters.

"You don't understand."

"Then explain it to me." She slides out of bed and stands in front of me, fully, gloriously naked. *Fuck.* "Explain why it is that we can't be together."

"You are Edward's—"

"He left me."

"He'll be back."

"You don't know that," she protests.

"You don't know Edward."

"And you do?"

"Better than you do."

"Somehow, I doubt that." She plants her hands on her hips, "You may've known the boy he once was, but I know the man he is now. The man who walked away from his calling because he—" Her voice fades. Her lips turn down.

"Exactly," I fold my arms across my chest, "he walked away from the Church for you. Do you really think he's not going to come back to you?"

"If he felt that much, why did he leave me in the first place?" She tips up her chin. "If he was that…into me, as you say, if he really felt something for me, why didn't he tell me so? Why didn't he stay and give me a chance to support him? To be with him? To help him work through things?" She throws up her hands. "Hell, why didn't he just come out and tell me how he felt about me?"

"Because love isn't that simple."

She firms her lips. "You're telling me?"

I stare at her flushed features, the stubborn set to her jaw, the resolve in her eyes, and blow out a sigh. "This was a mistake."

"What?" Her jaw drops.

"This." I point at the bed. "This should have never happened."

"Are you fucking kidding me?" she yells and I stiffen.

"I am very serious."

"So am I." She closes the distance between us and stabs a finger into my chest. "Are you seriously saying you regret what happened last night?"

"I regret," I swallow, "I regret letting things get this far between us. I should have stayed away. Shouldn't have allowed you to seduce me, I—"

"I seduced you? I…?" She shoves at my chest. "You're a jerk, you know that?"

Tell me about it. If this is the only way I can get her to stop thinking about me, if I can make her think I am enough of a douche —guaranteed, since I am… But if I allow her to see me that way, maybe she'll walk away. If she's angry enough with me, perhaps she'll never look at me again. Because, God forbid, one look from her, one touch... If she's anywhere in my vicinity, I won't be able to resist her.

So, I am a coward, that way. And what I am going to say is going to hurt her, but if it means it will put distance between us, then it's worth it. It's the only way to ensure that I, and that bastard Edward, can get through this with some semblance of a friendship alive between us.

If that means I am going to rip my heart out and pretend it never beat for her in the first place, then so be it.

"Now you know." I smirk, then draw myself up to my full height. "It was intense, babe. I'll give you that."

"Intense?" She scowls.

"Yeah, and your body...and your mouth...and man, that tight arse of yours... I'm glad I got to tap it when I could. In fact, I don't know of any other woman who enjoys anal as much as you do. It's what makes you special."

"I...it does?" She pales.

"Totally. One-hundred percent." I nod. "As for your pussy... So hot, so sweet, hell, I could write odes to it... But you know, you're not the only fish in the sea."

She opens and shuts her mouth. "What are you talking about? This is not like you Baron." Her lips tremble. "Why are you saying such hurtful things to me?"

"It's the truth."

"It's not."

"Unfortunately, yes." I bend my knees and peer into her eyes, "You see, I said and did what was needed so I could—"

"Get in my bed?"

I smile. "Knew you were smart. Knew there had to be a reason Edward was so hung up on you."

"Don't talk about him," she bursts out. "He was honorable. He wanted me enough to walk away from what was most important to him. Even when he left, he made sure I was taken care... If he'd only known what kind of a man you've turned into."

"And what kind is that?"

"A two-timing liar, who couldn't wait to bed the very woman

you'd been tasked with protecting." Her features grow stricken. "That's why you did it. You wanted to get back at him. You wanted to get revenge on him…for whatever went wrong between the two of you… Which is why you left in the first place."

"If that's what you think..." I raise my shoulders.

"It's not what I think. It's the truth." Her chest heaves. "Admit it. All of this was part of your plan so you could hurt Edward. So you could throw it in his face when he returns."

"Sure." My heart begins to thud. Sweat beads my palms. *Turn away from her. Get out of here while she's still upset.* So, she'll believe the worst of me. So, she'll never be tempted to come near me again. If I can't stick around long enough to be here for Edward, the least I can do is make sure that when he returns—and he will return—he has his woman to turn to.

"Good chat, babe," I pat her head, "but it's getting late and I know you must be anxious to get to work." I pivot, walk out of the bedroom and to the kitchen where I'd run a wash last night. Yeah, I'd managed to wake up long enough to do that, and a few other things, last night, before I'd crawled back into bed and arranged myself around her. I'd pulled her close, spooned her, thrown my leg about her, so every part of me was plastered to her, before I'd fallen asleep. The feel of her soft skin, her curves, the tiny noises of contentment she'd made as she'd cuddled close and slipped deeper into sleep— Yeah, good thing I have those memories to keep me going. It's all I am going to have… for I'm never going to meet another woman who'll affect me as much as she does.

I shake out my dry clothes, pull them on, then slip into the shoes I'd rescued from the shower last night. They're still damp, but what-fucking-ever. I can live with that… My heart though… How am I going to live without that?

I walk to the door, wrench it open and am about to step through, when footsteps sound behind me.

"Baron," she calls out and I pause. I want to look over my shoulder, want to see her face one last time. The delicate arch of her brow, the lushness of her lips, the curve of her shoulder. I shake my head.

No, no, no. If you see her, you'll lose the courage to leave her. It's best you walk away without a second glance. I square my shoulders, stay where I am.

"I'll never forgive you for this."

The hurt in her voice sinks into my veins. *Fuck. Fuck. Fuck.* I stare straight ahead, "You'll get over it, babe," I say without turning around, "just like I am already over you."

25

———————

*"The only person I feel comfortable around completely is my mother. I let my
emotions out with her, and for that I am thankful."*
-From Ava's Diary

Ava

"Jerk." I stare through the window of my bedroom at the SUV
parked across the street. Through the tinted glass, I can make out the
outline of the man inside, but not his rough-hewn features, not the
breadth of his shoulders, or how he seems to soak all of the oxygen in
the space.

Of course, the asshole is still there. God forbid that he break his
promise to his friend. Men. I snort. They'd stand by each other…
Make sure that no woman can come in between them… And me?
What about me? Where do I stand in all this? Nowhere. That's

where I am. He'd made that abundantly clear. So why am I still standing here, trying to catch a glimpse of him?

"What's wrong with me?" I turn away and begin to pace the living room. He'd flung that last comment at me, and I had been so shocked, I had allowed him to shut the door in my face. I'd rushed toward him, wanting to get the last word in, hoping that I could stop him, maybe. Maybe I'd held onto a sliver of hope that insisted that he was putting on an act...but...

No, he'd meant it. He'd meant every last, single, hurtful word that he'd carelessly tossed my way. *Shit, shit, shit.* How could I have allowed myself to become so entangled with this man? I'd allowed him into my life, into my heart. Shit. Tears well up and I wipe them away angrily. I will not cry over him. Will not. My face crumples. I turn around and walk into the bedroom, through to the bathroom and turn on the shower. I stand under the hot water, allowing it to pour over me. Soaking in the warmth, the comfort, the memory of the heat of his body that had curled around me, protecting me, cocooning me when he had last been in here with me. He'd held me, soothed me, rocked me, then carried me out of the cubicle and dried me.

He'd taken care of me...like he'd said he would... Only he hadn't. It had all been an act. Or had it? Damn the man, he had been so convincing. I had been sure that he felt something for me. But then again, what would I know about that? I have so little experience with men. No wonder, I thought I was in love with Edward. Maybe it's the speed with which things took place with him that made me mistake what I felt for him? Maybe I am not really sure what I feel for him... Or for Baron, for that matter. It's just, each time he'd fucked me...it had felt like more than just a shag... It had felt...as good as being with Edward. Shit. Why am I comparing the two of them? They are nothing alike... Except that they know each other. What are the odds, huh? The only two men I've slept with...know each other, hate each other, yet seem to care for each other.

But do either of them care about me?

I sleep with Edward and he leaves me. Then I fall into bed with Baron and he promptly decides to run away from me. Why is it that

I seem to be attracted to the same kind of man, and within such a short period of time? The kind who'll shag me, then fuck off at the first sign of feeling something for me? Is it me? Is there something wrong with me that these guys don't stick around?

I switch off the shower, dry myself, then put on my clothes. My phone pings. I walk over to my bedstand, pick up my phone and glance at the text message.

Raisa: *Have you made up your mind yet about coming to Dad's wedding?*

I stare at the message for another second. Have I made up my mind? No, no, I haven't. It still feels weird to refer to the upcoming event as Dad's wedding. He is my father. He was married to my mother. How can he be getting married again?

That's when the doorbell rings. Baron. It has to be him, right? I replace the phone on the bedstand, rush to the door, and open it. A stranger stands there. He's tall, and broad, his hair shaved close to his scalp. His features are hard, his gaze intense. A sense of danger clings to his shoulders. He should seem threatening, but strangely, he's not.

"Ava Erikson?"

I nod.

"I'm Archer, a friend and associate of Baron's." He tilts his head.

"Associate?" I blink. "What kind of associate?"

"We run a security business together."

Ah! That would explain why Baron seemed so nonchalant with the surveillance duties he had taken on. There's so much I don't about him, though. Not that I've had a chance to ask him about himself either. Every time we've been together, it seems like we've spent time arguing... Not to mention that crazy chemistry between us, which complicated everything. Hell, if I won't take every new piece of information I can get about him. Maybe it will help me understand him better?

"I am here to oversee a delivery." Archer prompts me.

"A delivery?" I frown, "I didn't order anything."

"It's definitely for you." The man's lips kick up in a smile that's not warm but not threatening either.

He moves aside to reveal two men hauling in a table between them.

"It's a table?" I blink.

"A dining table." He nods, "I was told it needed to be put in the kitchen."

"Kitchen?" I know I am gaping, but honestly, this is not what I expected first thing in the morning, and before I've even had my coffee.

"May I?" He gestures to the space behind me.

I move aside, watching as he directs the men to carry the dining table into the living room. They place it there, disappearing inside. I hear the sounds of them moving around, cleaning up the broken pieces of table and dishes. A few minutes later they re-appear, carrying the remnants of my stuff out to their truck, then the new table into the kitchen. They return to the truck for chairs and a large box—on the side of which is printed: *Wedgewood*. What the—? That's the name of an extremely upscale dinnerware brand, and trust me when I say that it's expensive. So, he's replacing all the crockery, my cheap-ass supermarket-bought crockery that he'd broken when he swept it off the table...because he was in a hurry to make love to me. My cheeks heat. I fold my arms around my waist, look on as a few minutes later, they wish me a good day and leave.

Meanwhile, Archer walks out of the house, reappears at the doorway, with a couple of bags of groceries.

"You bought me groceries?"

"Not me," He stabs his thumb in the direction of the SUV. "The big guy did."

"Oh."

Archer disappears inside the house. I pop my head around the doorway once again, take in the SUV with the tinted windows. Damn it, what are you up to, Baron? Why are you doing this?

I turn around, head to the kitchen, and find it spotless, a newer, better table and newer, better crockery, which Archer puts away for me. He also unloads the bags of groceries, putting perishable items in the fridge. It's surreal.

When he is finished, Archer turns to me. "Thank you for letting us into your home," he murmurs. "Sorry that we intruded."

"Oh, no." I shake my head in disbelief. "Thank you for, uh, cleaning up the mess."

"You're welcome." He shifts his weight between his feet. "There's one more thing," he mutters.

"Oh?"

"Baron asked me to take over as your security detail."

"Security detail?" I frown. "I don't need security."

"The last attack on you would suggest otherwise, Miss Erikson."

I stiffen. "You know about that?"

"Of course, I got a complete debriefing from him."

"Right." I bite the inside of my cheek. "So, if you're taking over, then does that mean that Baron — ?"

I rush away from him to the window and peer out to find the SUV is gone. In its place is a car I don't recognize. A hot sensation stabs at my chest. He's gone. He left me. He actually did it. So, he *did* mean everything he said? He really doesn't want me anymore?

"Miss Erikson?"

I turn to find Archer hovering in the doorway. "Please call me Ava, I insist."

"Ava," he smiles, "will you be leaving for work at the usual time?"

"Work?" I should go in. I need to keep the classes going. Now, more than ever, it is important to keep my routine going. I am not going to disrupt my life again for another man. Besides, I can't let my students down. And today is Friday, which means that I have four classes today. I nod. "I do have to head in, but not for a few hours yet."

He turns to leave and I stop him. "Archer," I call out, "how do you know Baron?"

He hesitates then turns to me. "We served in the army together. When I got out, I decided to work with him." He glances at the door, then back at me.

"I must be going now," he murmurs. "I'll wait for you outside."

He heads out and I lock the door behind him, head to the kitchen, and put on the kettle. While I am waiting for it to boil, I walk toward the fridge and check out what he brought—fresh vegetables, cheese, milk. On the counter, I find apples, bananas, bread. Everything is marked as being ethically-sourced and organic. There's even a box of cereal—the one I like—and a few bars of chocolate, my favorite brand.

Wow, he'd certainly put a lot of thought into this. How does he know what brand of cereal I like to eat, or what my favorite brand of chocolate is? Had he simply guessed it or had he seen evidence of it in my kitchen already, and known what to buy?

When the kettle boils, I pour the hot water onto a tea bag in a mug, then carry it over to the dining table. My brand-new dining table. I grab the carton of milk from the fridge, pour a little into my tea.

Why is he being this attentive? And after he'd insulted me, then walked out on me. He may claim he doesn't want me, but he does care for me. Of course, he does. So why had he behaved so horribly toward me? It's almost like he wants me to hate him. Is that what this is? Does he want me to think that he doesn't want anything to do with me, so I'll stay away from him?

I head inside my bedroom, grab the phone from where it's been plugged into the socket… Something I don't remember doing. So, it must have been Baron who did it. Hmmm. I sink down on the bed. Why would he anticipate my needs one minute, and the next, turn around and tell me he's already forgotten about me? Gah! It makes no sense.

Later that evening, I sink into a comfortable chair in Summer and Sinclair's townhouse.

Archer had driven me to work, then brought me here. I'd told him he could leave, that I could take the tube home, but of course, he wasn't having any of it. He'd told me that Mr. Masters had ordered him to stay with me at all times. Ugh! Of course, Baron had to have a strong dominant surname. And of course, I had allowed him to fuck me in the arse, without even finding out what his full name was. I hunch my shoulders.

What does that say about me? Am I doomed to forever fall for the wrong man? Am I such a slut that one whiff of the right peen and I can't think of anything but how to get it between my legs? My core clenches and my toes curl. And boy, oh, boy, both peens had been works of art. Big and thick and broad enough to stretch me in the most delicious way possible... *Gah, stop that.*

"Ava?" Victoria has a concerned look on her face. "You okay?"

"Yes, of course." I shake my head to clear it, as if that's going to help. I can still smell Baron's dark scent, feel the hardness of his chest pressed against my back as he'd bent over me and —

"Ava!" Isla snaps her fingers in front of me.

"What?" I jerk. "What happened?"

"Apparently, Baron happened," she drawls.

"Stop that," I scold her. "Uh, can I get something to drink?"

"Of course." Summer pours frozen margarita into a soup bowl — erm, I mean, a glass — and hands it to me. No, seriously, these are so huge I have to wrap both of my hands around the circumference of the glass to hold it up... Just like I had wrapped my fingers around his dick and —

"Hello, earth to Ava," Isla sing-songs.

I frown at her. "Yes, yes, I am listening."

"Are you, though?" She scowls. "Your head seems to be somewhere else... Maybe the rest of your body too?" She smirks.

"Oh, shut up." I bring the glass to my mouth, sip it. The fruity taste of melon and strawberries, laced with the pungent kick of the tequila, fills my palate. "Yum," I smack my lips, "these are deadly."

"Enjoy." Victoria raises her mocktail glass.

"Have another on my behalf." Karina nods.

"You're not drinking." I frown.

"No, and no I am not pregnant...yet," she continues, "but yeah, I am trying and," she raises her shoulders, "it's no secret that I want a baby so badly that I tried to get artificially inseminated —"

"Instead, thanks to Arpad, you found that doing it the real way is more fun." Julia laughs.

"Oh, you have no idea." Karina's eyes twinkle.

"I do, actually," Summer mutters. "It was a lot of fun…but wait until the morning sickness kicks in." She shakes her head. "It can be a bummer."

"I know, right?" Victoria turns to me. "Thankfully, I haven't suffered too much, but apparently, for some women it lasts the entire pregnancy, and—" She squeaks, "Wait, what? You're pregnant too?"

Summer beams, her features lighting up.

"OMG!" Julia jumps to her feet and rushes over to Summer, "You're having a baby? Oh, wow!" She hugs Summer, who laughs.

"Yeah, I only just found out," she says. "I couldn't wait to tell you guys."

"Congratulations," Karina walks over to her, "I am so excited for you, Summer, I really am."

"Thank you." Summer turns to Karina. She takes Karina's hand between both of hers. "Your turn will come, I promise."

"I am sure it will, if Arpad has anything to do with it," she mutters.

Summer laughs. "Enjoy it, babe. Once you're pregnant, he'll change."

"What do you mean?" Karina frowns.

"I mean, he'll want to wrap you up in cotton wool—"

"Unlike the ropes he prefers to use right now?"

There's silence in the room, then the women burst out laughing.

"Okay, enough." My cheeks heat. "TMI, you guys, TMI."

"Says the woman who's managed to bang not one, but two, of the Seven." Isla turns to me. "It has to be a record of sorts, right?"

"Wait." Amelie turns to me. "What did I miss? I though you and Edward…" Her voice trails off. "It *is* you and Edward, right?"

She hesitates and my cheeks heat.

"Yeah, it was me and Edward," I mumble.

"But it isn't anymore," Isla pipes up.

I shoot her a dirty look.

Summer shushes Isla, "Seriously, Iz, sometimes you don't know when to zip it."

"Correction," Isla's shoulders hunch, "I never know when to zip it." She looks at me with a pleading expression on her face, "Sorry, Ava, didn't mean to dump your stuff out there."

I blow out a breath. "It's fine. I mean, what the hell? The rest of you know about it already, so…" I turn to Amelie, "I slept with Baron."

"Baron?" She frowns. "One of the Seven? The one who just returned…?" She blinks at me rapidly. "Oh." She nods, then her gaze widens. "OH," she coughs, "you slept with Baron."

"Yeah." I drain the margarita, reach over and top up my glass. "Now you guys know all my dirty secrets. Not that there was much to begin with. At least, there hadn't been till a few weeks ago. You know, all I had was a crazy crush on Edward."

"You mean, the Father?" Karina prompts.

"No," I frown at her, "I mean, he's called Edward and also sparkles in the sunlight, but I'm talking about Edward the vampire—"

"Vampire?" Julia's gaze widens. "A real-life vampire?"

Isla frowns at her, "No silly, she means Edward from Twilight."

"Twilight?" Amelie repeats. "What do you mean, like dusk, dawn, twilight?"

"Not quite," Victoria pipes up. "I think she means, like Breaking Dawn Twilight."

"How can it be twilight when it's dawn?" Amelie's forehead furrows, "Unless it's a figure of speech I am not aware of, in which case—"

"I'm talking about *Twilight*, the book," I clarify.

"Unless you are talking about twilight-themed cupcakes which, I assure you, I am good at baking," she goes on as if she didn't hear me. "In fact, I think I should create an entire new range of sparkly cupcakes to celebrate baby showers." Amelie snaps her fingers, "It's a great idea." She reaches over, wraps her arm around me and kisses my cheek. "You are a genius, Ava."

"I am?"

"It's exactly what I was looking for as a means to differentiate my pastry business in the marketplace."

Like that clarified anything?

"Right." I manage. "You really haven't heard of *Twilight*?"

She stares at me, as if I am crazy. "Of course, I know about *Twilight*." She waves a hand in the air. "It's just, I need to call my team right now and get a plan in place. Twilight-themed cupcakes, ha!" She rubs her hands together. "It's a brilliant idea." She kisses me again on both cheeks, then brushes past me to grab her bag. "I gotta get going. You guys don't mind, right?"

I stare, bemused, as she hitches her massive tote over her shoulder. She heads for the door, then pauses and turns to me, "Oh, and if I were you, I'd enjoy the one who is still with you. Unless, of course, you'd prefer to keep both," she smirks, "in which case, I wouldn't blame you." She blows me a kiss and heads for the door, which slams behind her.

O-k-a-y. I turn back to my margarita, my cheeks burning. Shit, of all the girls here, I know Isla the best. I'd met the others through her, and they had pretty much adopted me into their circle. But they've known the Seven much longer than me. What the hell must they think of me now? I clear my throat, "Uh, guess I'd better head off now."

"Oh, no you don't, woman." Summer grabs hold of me and steers me over into a chair. "You sit." She jabs a finger at me. "You're not going anywhere until you share all the juicy details."

"You mean all the details of the train wreck that my life is turning out to be, right?" I mutter under my breath.

"Stop that." Isla frowns at me. "No one here is judging you, Ava."

Except me. I'm judging myself. But that's my issue, right?

Summer walks over with another full glass of margarita, "Here you go."

She turns away to sink onto the couch near me. "So… Baron, hmm?" She waggles her eyebrows at me.

"Yeah, well, it's not how it looks." Gah, what a clichè I am turning out to be. I take another gulp of the margarita, which goes down smoothly. Lick my lips, then stare around at the faces of the girls. "What?" I frown.

"Deets, babe, the spicy, juicy deets." Isla leans forward in her chair, "How was it?"

"I am not telling you," I say, horrified. "Besides, who are you talking about?" I glance at her from under lowered eyelashes, "Edward or Baron?"

"Omigod!" Isla fans herself. "Bitch here gets all the dick and she's still complaining. Better two cocks than zero shafts, babe."

"Iz," I laugh, "your mouth will get you into so much trouble someday."

"Here's hoping." She drains her glass, reaches for the pitcher on the table in the center, "So…which one?" She tilts her head in my direction, "Or are you going to keep both?"

"What?" I choke on my margarita. "What are you talking about?"

Summer reaches over to smack me on the back. "Why, what's wrong with having two at the same time?"

"I couldn't," I gape at her. My cheeks heat. "I mean, I shouldn't, I mean… It's not how it's done."

"But you want to?" Karina drawls from her perch on the chair opposite me. "Do you want to keep them both?"

"No. Yes. I don't know." I shake my hair back from my face. "I mean, come on, this is real life, people. You don't go around bedding and staying in a relationship with two men. And to be fair, I only hooked up with Baron after Edward left." Okay, so it was immediately after Edward left, like he departed stage right and Baron walked in from the other side, but whatever.

"So, do you still have feelings for Edward?" Summer asks softly.

I chew the inside of my cheek. "Do I still want him? Yes, I do. At least, I think I do. I mean, I saw him and it was like love at first sight. I couldn't get him out of my head. And Baron? Well, there's something about him that's so compelling, almost hypnotic. There's an edginess to him, and an anger that's alluring. Edward broke his vows for me…and Baron… Well, he doesn't want my vows, so right now, I have neither, it would seem."

"Oh, babe." Isla places her glass down on the side table, then walks over and bends to hug me. "I am so sorry. Men can be cunts, you know that?"

"Yeah, only he was good to my cunt. Well, they both were, to be fair."

Isla chuckles. "At least, you got good sex out of it."

"There is that."

"You are two up on me, not that I was ever going to hook up with any of the Seven."

"No, you went for the bigger, meaner, older brother to one of the Seven instead," Karina mutters.

Isla straightens and flicks her hair over her shoulder, "Oh, please. I hated the man on sight, and now I am going to have to see him almost every day, when the wedding rehearsals begin."

"Rehearsals?" I frown.

"The bridezilla—and this one is the mother of them all—insists on at least three before the actual wedding."

"As long as you are getting paid..." Karina interjects.

"You bet, I am," Isla bares her teeth, "and it's all Liam's money so there is that, but enough about me." She turns to survey me down the length of her nose. "What are you going to do now, Missy?"

"Me?" I take another huge sip of the margarita and hiccough. Oops. I scowl up at her. "For now, I am not doing anything. Except staying clear of men."

"What if Baron changes his mind and wants you back?"

"He can go fuck himself," I mutter. "After the way he walked out on me, it's going to take more than just apologies for me to be with him." But damn, if I don't still want to fuck him... Only, my emotions are already involved here... If I slept with him again, it would become something I couldn't walk away from.

"And Edward?" Karina asks. "What about him?"

"What about him?" I glance at her. "He left me; end of story."

"He'll be back."

"So, everyone keeps saying."

"As their security consultant, I am privy to the affairs of all the Seven" she murmurs, "and based on what I know, I can tell you the Seven don't like loose ends. Not that you are a loose end...." She hastens to add, "But you know what I mean?"

"No," I place the glass on the table, "I don't, actually. What are you trying to say?"

"Just that, chances are, Edward will return, and sooner, rather than later. What are you going to do then?"

I contemplate the depths of my glass. "I have no idea." I stare around the faces of my friends, before settling on Karina, "What would you do?"

She shakes her head. "Oh, no, no. You are putting me on the spot."

"No, I really want to know." I lean forward, "I am so confused; it will help me to get another perspective."

"I am probably the wrong person to ask," she mutters. "I am not the conventional, roll over and submit to a guy kind of gal... Well, none of us are, actually." She looks around the room. "And one thing I have learned is that, fuck society. No one knows your situation and what you are facing, so no one needs to understand your decisions. It's you who needs to follow your instincts."

"And what if my instincts are muddled? What if I can't figure out what to do?"

"Then it means you are not ready to decide. It means," she smiles gently, "that you wait."

"For how long, though?" Not that I am in any hurry, but hell, if it wouldn't help to figure out where I stand in this sorry mess.

"Until you're ready."

"When will I be ready?"

She chuckles. "You'll know when you know."

Julia's phone buzzes, she glances at it, and a smile tugs her lips. "On that note... And not that I want to break this up, guys, and don't think I am leaving because hubby texted me...but—"

"Oh, please." Isla scoffs, "Just go, already. I mean, all you guys are so in love that it's making me sick." She makes a gagging noise.

I laugh. "Don't worry, I am right there with you, Iz."

"But... I do have to go, too." Isla looks over at me with regret. "I have a ton of things to prep for my upcoming weddings. Best I get home, so I can get an early start tomorrow."

"Okay," I rise to my feet, "I'd better get going too."

26

Baron

I pause in front of Saint's townhouse at Primrose Hill.

After I'd briefed Archer on Ava's schedule, I'd made it to my loft —which I hadn't been to since I'd met Ava—showered and shaved. Then made a few more calls, this time to my contacts to find out who could have been behind the men who'd attacked Ava. The information hadn't looked good.

It had confirmed to me what I'd already suspected. I need the help of the rest of the Seven. The situation is more serious than I'd imagined and I need my friends to back me up on my plan. I hate to ask them for help, but if this is the only way to keep Ava safe, I'll do it. I'd gladly sacrifice my life for her if it came to it... Only, this is harder. Meeting my friends face-to-face, asking them to back me up. Sweat beads my palm. I shift the folder I am carrying to my other hand, rub my palm on my pants, then raise it to knock on the door, when it swings open.

Weston, stands in the doorway, his face wreathed in a big smile.

"Baron!" He grabs my arm and hauls me in for a hug. I stand stiffly, while he thumps my back, "I still can't believe you are back among us."

"Me neither," I mutter.

He releases me, then steps back and peers into my face. "You don't look like you got much sleep, though."

"You don't say." I scowl.

Motherfucker looks freshly scrubbed, his skin glowing with health. He's wearing a beard, which he hadn't had when we were younger. Of course, that was years ago. I am still getting used to seeing the physical changes in my friends. Emotionally and mentally, though, they are still the same. Which means, all of them have the intelligence of a twelve-year-old—collectively.

Weston's smile widens. Shit, doesn't the man have anything better to do than look happy at the world? And content? Yeah, it comes off of him in waves. He reeks of happiness and fulfillment and all those emo words that I'd never have associated with any of the Seven. But then, I'd have never thought that I'd fall for a woman who was taken either... So yeah, shit happens.

I brush past him and walk inside. "So," I clear my throat, "I take it Saint doesn't know that I am coming to this little reunion?"

"He'll come around." Weston claps my back. "You know Saint. His bark is more dangerous than his bite."

"No, actually. I don't." I scowl. "The last few times I've met him, he's made it clear he doesn't want anything to do with me."

"Yeah." Weston's smile diminishes in wattage. Thank fuck. He was beginning to creep me out with all that happiness pouring off of him. There should be a law against any of the Seven being in such good spirits. I mean, it's practically written—somewhere—that the Seven needed to be growly, grumpy alphaholes, like me. So, to see them jovial and chilled out, like the proverbial cat that swallowed the canary, or in this case, like men who've found the loves of their lives, is disconcerting, to say the least.

"Saint's a bit of a complex character," Weston offers.

"Aren't we all?"

"Good thing Edward's not here. This way, you only have to deal with one pissed off wanker at a time—"

I shoot him a glance and he winces. "Oops, sorry, slip of the tongue. I didn't mean to—"

"It's fine," I drawl, "I am not going to collapse bawling if you speak about E."

"You're the only guy who was close enough to Ed to call him that."

"I'm also the only one who dared challenge him when he said he was going to join the seminary," I mutter.

"You knew him better than we did."

"None of you guys dissuaded him, either."

"He was hell bent on it." Weston frowns. "Considering what we went through, if that was what brought him some measure of peace then…" he shrugs, "who were we to step in between him and his calling?"

"Calling." I snort. "He was running away from facing his demons."

"Like you did." A new voice cuts in.

I turn to find Saint prowling toward us.

"You were saying?" I scowl.

"That you were the one who abandoned us."

"I joined the army," I snap.

"Without telling any of us."

"Didn't think it mattered, either way."

Saint closes the distance between us so quickly that I blink. He grabs my collar, hauls me up, "If you had only cared enough to open your eyes and see how your leaving was going to impact the rest of us. If you had only thought of anyone else except yourself."

"I did," I say through gritted teeth, "It's why I left, you tosser."

"Is that your excuse?" he growls. "That you were too shaken by everything that happened? That you couldn't cope with it? That you didn't have the balls to share your decision with everyone? No, you upped and got out... You decided not to stay in touch, except for your stupid snail mail letters—which was a bad decision, by the way. It's what helped us track you down, you bastard."

"I wasn't trying to hide." I raise my shoulders. "I simply wanted my space."

"No, you *thought* you needed space, when in reality, you were too afraid."

"Afraid?" I scowl. "What the hell are you talking about?"

"You were afraid of your feelings. Afraid to feel any kind of connection with any of us. Afraid that if you, for one moment, stopped and allowed yourself to feel, that you would—"

"What?" I snap. "What would happen if I allowed myself to feel?"

"You'd have felt compelled to stay back and actually develop some kind of a relationship with the rest of us. Not to mention, you'd have been forced to sort out your shit with Edward and—"

"Enough," I break away from him, "this was a bad idea." I pivot and head for the doorway. "I shouldn't have come here."

"That's right, run away." Saint's voice follows me. "When the going gets tough, you always did do a Baron."

"Do a Baron?" I pause. "What the hell does that mean?"

"You know, losing your balls. Not having the courage to stand up and fight for what you believe in."

"You want to fight?" I reel around and confront him, "Want to get your arse handed to you, is that it?"

He laughs, "I'm faster than you, stronger than you, leaner than you, you arse."

"But you're pussy-whipped."

"And you aren't?" He smirks.

"I don't have a wife and a kid on the way to worry about."

"No, you're too much of a coward to commit to anyone."

"Is that what you think?"

"What other explanation is there?" He shrugs. "Not that it matters, to be honest. I am sick of this shit, anyway. You come home and everyone celebrates, as if you're a vanquishing hero. Little do they know how much of a weakling you really are."

"Weakling, huh?" I glance around, then place the folder on a coffee table nearby. I straighten, curl my fingers into fists, "Let's take this outdoors, shall we?"

27

Baron

"Actually, let's not." Saint rushes toward me. Asshole swings with his fist, catches me under the chin. My head snaps back; pain squeezes the backs of my eyes. My vision wavers. I shake my head to clear it, straighten but he's already in my face again. He lands a punch in my side, then the other, in my shoulder, back to my stomach. My body protests, my shoulder screams, and the breath screeches out of me. I lurch forward, throw my arm around him, and we hug each other in the semblance of an embrace that isn't really one. He punches me in the side, and again, as I lean the bulk of my weight on him. He staggers back, and I shove at him, my shoes squeaking on the floor as I propel the both of us toward the back of the room. I lean back, swing, catch him under his chin. Blood spurts out as he tumbles back into the wet bar. The force of his momentum carries him over. At the last moment, he grabs my collar and the impetus carries me along. I crash to the floor, his body knocks into me, and the bottles from the shelves above rain down on us. A bottle from the top-most shelf teeters over, then plunges down toward us, and I throw my arms around his head to shield him. The bottle hits the back of my hand, bounces off. I grunt as pain whips up my arm.

We stay that way for a few seconds. Another glass rolls over the counter, falls over to the other side. The crash echoes through the space, then there's silence. The scent of alcohol deepens. Puddles of liquor surround us, dotted with broken glass shards.

Saint pushes me off of him and staggers to his feet, pieces of broken glass sliding off of him. He holds out his hand. I stare at it, then up at him.

"Thanks," he grumbles. "You protected me from getting hurt."

I firm my lips, then nod. I grab his hand and he hauls me to my feet.

"You guys okay?" Weston asks from the other side of the bar. "Figured it was best to let you chaps fight it out."

"What happened here?" Arpad walks in, followed by Damian and Sinclair.

"Thought we heard the sound of breaking glass." Damian glances around the space.

"Guess you guys were getting reacquainted?" Sinclair drawls.

"How did you guess?" I say wryly.

"So, what's the verdict?" Weston interjects. "You guys kissed and made up yet?"

We glare at each other.

Damian side-steps a broken bottle, then leans his elbow on a clear patch of the bar counter. "Or, if you want to go another round—"

"That won't be necessary," Saint snaps.

I tilt my head.

He blows out a breath. "Much as I hate to be beholden to you for anything, seems you did protect me from getting badly hurt."

"I'll pay for the damages," I offer stiffly.

"That won't be necessary," he retorts.

"So, you guys gonna shake or what?" Arpad glances at his watch, "I gotta get out of here in half an hour."

"Newlyweds." Sinner tsks.

"Better enjoy it before the kids come along." Damian chuckles.

Arpad scowls at them. "Relax, you guys. Let me enjoy my time with my new bride without all of you getting on my balls."

I snicker. "Oh, she has you by the balls all right, brother."

"Look who's talking." Arpad smirks. "You're in as much trouble as the rest of us, ol' chap."

"Hey, hey," I hold up my hands, "I came here on a work thing, so can we get to that?"

"Once you shake," Damian insists. "Go on," he urges me, "get it over with so we can get to what you want to discuss."

"Yeah, fine." I roll my shoulders, grab Saint's hand. We shake.

Saint jerks his chin. "I'll be watching you."

"Just as long as you can help me keep an eye on her."

"Thought you were doing that?" He frowns.

"Yeah, about that..." I shuffle my feet.

He releases my hand, fixes me with an impenetrable gaze. "What's up?" He scowls. "It must be something very important that made you walk in here and make peace."

"I wasn't the one who harbored hard feelings," I remind him.

He looks like he is about to protest, then nods. "I still haven't forgiven you for what you did, but if your woman is in danger..."

"Not my woman," I snap.

Saint stares at me, then his face cracks in a smile.

I stare, "That wasn't a joke, you wanker."

Saint bends, then pulls out a bottle of Macallan's from under the bar. He pushes the broken glass pieces to the side, slams the bottle on the table. Damian grabs a few glasses from the far end of the bar, lines them on the counter. Saint tops up the glasses, then hands me one.

"What are we drinking to?" I ask suspiciously.

He jerks the glass in my direction, and I accept it as the others reach for their drinks.

"Well?" I scowl, "Are you going to tell me or keep smiling like a maniac?"

Saint chuckles, "You heard that, guys?" He turns to the other men, "Seems another one of us is getting ready to bite the dust."

"The only one who's going to have a mouthful of dust is you, if you don't knock off your cryptic comments."

"It bothers you, huh?" Saint snatches up his own glass. "Being vulnerable and open, knowing your heart could be shattered any moment?"

"You're wrong, my heart can't be hurt anymore."

"Oh?" He scowls. "Why's that?"

Because it doesn't belong to me anymore, is what I want to say. Instead, I sip from the glass. The liquid burns its way down, and heat infuses my veins. "Because," I tip up my chin and stare at him, "I am not going back on my word to Edward."

Damian tosses back his drink, places the glass on the counter, "Ever occur to you that Edward called you and asked you for this favor as a way of bringing you two together?

"What do you mean?" I frown. "That he purposely put us together, as a test?"

"More as a way of getting the two of you to get to know each other?"

"Why would he do that?" I frown. "It makes no sense."

"Maybe he did it subconsciously?" Weston offers. "After all, the two of you were close."

"More like, after what we went through, we couldn't stand the sight of each other," I say wryly.

"What did you go through?" Arpad leans forward on the balls of his feet. "Neither of you has ever spoken about what happened to you during the incident."

I stiffen, then draw myself up to my full height. "It's best kept that way."

"If you don't talk about it, it's not going to help you heal," Weston warns.

"If I do talk about it, it's only going to dredge up a whole lot of shit that I am better off without."

Sinner shakes his head. "That's what I thought. Then, I met Summer and realized, turning your back on your feelings is a one-way trip to hell."

"A place I am well acquainted with," I mutter.

"It doesn't have to be that way." Sinner leans forward. "Let us help you."

"You can," I glance around at the faces of my friends, "by helping me track down who attacked Ava."

"Hangonabloodysecond," Saint bursts out. "Someone attacked her?"

"Why do you think I am here?" I reach for the bottle of whiskey and top myself up. "It happened last night, after she left the restaurant."

"Thought you were keeping watch over her?"

"Yeah," I rub the back of my neck, "she was on a date and I—"

"You lost your cool." Saint scowls. "It happens."

"Edward met her first," I mumble. "I shouldn't feel this way about her."

"You can't control who you develop feelings for," Weston interjects. "Trust me, all of us here have tried to resist and failed."

Damian nods. "We each had to go through some crazy shit before we could face our emotions, but once we did? Boy, was it all clear."

"Easy for you to say." I glower at him. "When you met your woman, was she already in a relationship with someone else?"

"Victoria was," Saint says slowly. "She'd just buried her husband, but he hadn't been her husband, in the real sense of the word."

"Well, whatever it was between Edward and Ava, it was very real." I squeeze my fingers around my glass. "It's why he asked me to watch out for her."

"He's not here," Saint points out. "You are."

"What are you trying to say, man?" I frown. "I can't betray Edward."

Except, I already have, and fuck, if I am going to let it happen again.

"All's fair..." Saint bares his teeth. "Edward took off. You did the honorable thing; you came back to help someone in need. You were there for her when she needed you. If the two of you develop feelings for each other, well, that's just the way it is."

"If only everything was that simple."

"It's as simple or as complicated as you make it out to be." His lips twist. "A word of advice from me, ol' chap?"

"Not that I care about what you're going to say, but don't let that stop you."

"I won't." Saint's smile widens. "After everything you've been through, you have a chance at being happy. It doesn't often happen that you meet someone who brings out the best part of you—which in your case is especially a rarity, given those parts are particularly hard to find—" he smirks. "So, if I were you, I wouldn't let the fact that she and Edward had a thing stop you."

"He left the Church for her," I snap.

"You faced your fears for her." He grips my shoulder. "You came back to a life that you hadn't been able to face, made up with your friends, put her needs before yours. Even now, you're thinking of her first. I'd say you have as much right as him to pursue her."

"What are you saying?"

"He means," Sinner drawls, "go after the fair maiden. Let her decide who she wants."

"Agreed." Damian nods.

Arpad jerks his chin.

Weston scowls. "You have to do what is right for you, man."

"And you?" I raise my tumbler in his direction, "What would you do if you were in my shoes?"

"Me?" He scratches his chin. "I'd go after what was mine." He looks me up and down, "Is she yours, Baron?"

I glare at him and he chuckles. "Thought so," He raises a shoulder, "The way I see it, you don't have a choice, man. You're going to have to follow your heart, and well, the rest is not in your hands anyway."

I stare into the dregs of the amber liquid in my glass. Are they right? Is it that simple? Am I over-complicating everything by my sense of right and wrong? My instincts are the only thing that kept me from getting killed in the army. It's what had led me to staying away from my friends. The same instincts which had known when it was time to return when Edward called... Which now tells me, the only thing worth living for is her. That if I'm not with her, if I don't use this opportunity that had been handed to me, I am a fool.

She wants me, she's made it clear. She still has feelings for Edward… But hell, it's true that I am here and he isn't. I hadn't meant to fall for her… I am not at fault here. He turned his back on her; he passed off his responsibility to me—and I intend to do what is in her best interests. Which is…allow her to see how it could be with me. The guys are right. Ultimately, it isn't in my hands who she chooses. All I can do is allow her to make the decision. It isn't mine to make. I can't force her to choose by default. If I respect her, I should allow her to decide for herself. And I do. I trust her to make this choice for herself.

I turn to Saint, hold out my hand. "I hate saying it, but you're right."

He smirks, bypasses my hand, to pull me into a hug. "I always am."

"What-bloody-ever." I thump his back, then step back, and glance around the room.

"There's one other thing I could do with some help on."

"What's that?" Arpad asks.

"The man Edward hurt," I brush past Saint, walk around the bar and step over the broken glass pieces to face the other men, "he hasn't woken up yet, so there are no clues forthcoming as to his identity; though I swear I have seen him somewhere before." I shake my head, "I just can't place him, though."

"You think he's connected with the attack on Ava?" Sinclair flicks dust off his £7000 suit jacket. No matter the occasion, he is always dressed like he has a bloody board meeting to attend. Me? I can't stand ties, or collars, for that matter. No wonder Edward fits right in with these guys. He constrains himself with his duty to the Lord—or at least, he used to do so. And the rest of the Seven, with the exception of our resident rock star Damian? They don't think twice about knotting a tie around their neck… If the occasion demands it. I'd rather face a bullet than do that. Oh, Wait, I had faced a bullet… many bullets, rather than risk being stuck in a nine-to-five existence, or any kind of relationship, for that matter. And now I am willingly looking to embrace conventions... Only for her. If this is the only way to keep her safe? Then I'll gladly do so.

"Seems too much of a coincidence, don't you think?" I tilt my head.

"Now that you mention it." Sinclair widens his stance. "You think he's connected with the Mafia?"

"I know he is." I fold my arms across my chest. "It's why the normally controlled Father lost his composure. The man told him that he is linked to our kidnapping."

"How?" Damian scowls, "Did Edward mention any details?"

"He mentioned that the bastard was at St. Lucian's with us."

"What?" Saint exclaims. "Asshole was a fellow student? You think he shared information about us with the kidnappers?"

"Apparently." I nod.

"What else?" Arpad growls. "What else did Edward tell you?"

"He also said that he hadn't been in control of himself, which is why he'd lost his temper." I rub the back of my neck. "When he realized the man had helped perpetuate the incident and that he was still involved with the Mafia, he hadn't been able to stop himself. In fact, Edward had been sure that he'd killed the man. It was only when I went to the church and found his body, I realized he was still breathing."

"Did Edward mention where he was headed?" Saint interjects.

"Would you?" I narrow my gaze on him and Saint scowls.

"That's a no, then."

"And there's no way to contact him," Damian murmurs, "which means, there's no way for Ed to know that the man survived the attack."

"Do you think that's why he left," Sinclair turns to me, "because he thought he'd killed the man?"

"Among other things." I walk over to the coffee table, retrieve the folder with the pictures of the mystery man, then hand it over to Sinclair. "Thought I'd share his pictures, in case any of you recognize him."

Sinclair opens the folder, takes in the pictures. His gaze narrows, he flicks through the pictures, then stares up at me.

"What?" I frown. "You recognize him?"

"I swear I've seen him before, but I can't place where."

Arpad walks over to Sinclair, takes the pictures from him. "Shit, I know him, he's the homeless guy I got into a fight with. Bastard had video on his phone of Karina walking up the steps of the Town Hall to get married."

"He did?" I frown.

"That's right." Sinclair snaps his fingers. "He used to sit in front of my office building. I am sure I put money into his hat a few times."

"Homeless guy?" Saint walks around the bar, snatches up one of the pictures from Arpad. "What the hell?" he swears. "I saw him in front of the Dorchester when I was with Victoria."

"So, let me get this straight," I glance around the group, "He's had encounters with each of you?"

"I didn't meet him," Damian says slowly, "but he must be the person whom Julia had a conversation with." Damian glances up from the picture he'd taken from Arpad. "She mentioned that a homeless guy had shown her his phone with the video of the song I'd recorded as an apology to her. It's what made her change her mind about me, you know. In a way, I owe my being reunited with Julia to him."

"And if he hadn't shown me the video of Karina heading up the steps of the town hall, I'd have never made it in time to stop her wedding." Arpad adds.

"He also had a signboard, on which he'd scrawled some poem from Byron."

"I noticed that too." Saint growls, "Asshole asked me for a cigarette, which I didn't have. Bet he ate at the soup kitchen at my hotel every night, too."

I turn to Saint, "So did he help you in anyway?"

"Not unless you count the fact that Victoria felt sorry for him, and I told her the same thing, that he probably ate at the pop-up soup kitchen my hotel hosts every night with the leftovers."

"Which made her look at you in a different light?" I surmise.

"If you mean that he humanized me?" He raises a shoulder, "I guess so, probably."

"And you Sinclair?" I tilt my head in his direction, "He help you with your love life?"

"I should bloody well hope not," Sinclair drawls, "though after I got together with Summer, I never saw him again."

"And what about you Weston?" I turn my gaze on him, "He help you too?"

"I noticed he was barefoot and gave him my shoes. Then when Amelie asked me about them, I told her what I'd done." He scowls. "Guess he showed me in a favorable light, as well."

"He helped bring out the man behind the alphahole, again," I muse.

"What are you thinking, Baron?" Arpad turns to me, "You think he played some kind of cupid for all of us, helping us get together with our women?"

"That may be stretching things a bit, but yeah… I am thinking something along those lines. You have to admit that it's somewhat dodgy that the guy shows up at a pivotal moment for each of you, then seems to disappear from your sight when you guys get hitched."

"So what?" Weston rubs the back of his neck. "He's a well-wisher?"

And hell, if I couldn't do with some additional help in getting my woman. I shake my head. Now, that is fanciful thinking. I don't need anybody else's advice. I've got this. I'll find a way to make up for the way I'd acted with Ava. I have to.

"And you?" Sinner frowns at me, "where have you seen him before?"

"I don't know." I drag my fingers through my hair. "I am sure I have seen him before, although I feel like he was younger at the time." I raise my shoulders. "Either way, when he regains conscious-ness, I plan to be there to question him. Meanwhile," I turn to the guys, "I need to get to my woman."

28

"My mum always told me that I'm perfect, that I'm beautiful and that no guy deserves me. But how much of what she says is lies? Is it a lie if she believes it's true? Is it possible to tell the truth and lie simultaneously?"
-From Ava's Diary

Ava

Half an hour after leaving Summer and Sinclair's townhouse, the car pulls up outside a fast-food outlet. I'd left their place and realized I didn't want to go home yet. Especially not, since the place reminds me of Baron.

Everywhere I look, I see him—on the couch, in the shower, in the kitchen, in my bed. Shit, it's like his presence is woven into every room there. Also, it had been so long since I'd danced…just for the pleasure of dancing…. Just being able to move to the music without worrying about anything else. Yeah, it's exactly what I need. I want to get to my studio, and I want to do it unaccompanied by Baron's watchdog. The man has no claim on me. I don't need his bloody protection. I am a free, independent woman who can do what I want, when I want, and no man is going to take that from me. I am going to get to the studio, and on my own steam. Which means I have to ditch Archer. So, I ask him to stop at the fast-food outlet.

I get out of the car, and so does Archer.

"I don't need you to accompany me in there," I point out.

He shakes his head, "Baron said—"

"Yeah, yeah, I know what he said, but surely, I am safe in there." I point to the outlet. "You can see everyone who comes in and out of it."

He hesitates and I throw up my hands, "Come on. Surely, I deserve a bit of privacy, a few minutes of being able to eat my food in peace?"

He firms his lips, then nods. "Five minutes, then I'll come in there."

"Fifteen minutes."

"Ten," he folds his arms across his chest, "and that's about all I can agree to."

"Deal." I sniff, then turn and stomp inside the outlet. I place my order, glance through the shop window to find him standing to attention, his gaze fixed on me. Shit, this isn't working, I need to find a way to give him a slip. Just then, a gang of students walks into the shop. They mill around, chattering, pointing to the menu board on the wall. They press in closer to the counter, cutting me off from his sight.

Instantly, I spin around, walk to the door at the back. I pass the kitchen, travel down a short corridor, reach the door at the back and twist it open. I walk down the alley. Reaching the main road, I turn left, head for the tube station. Good thing I am wearing sneakers and jeans. It means I can run. I hit the tube station, make it to the tills and the platform. I glance back, half convinced that I'll see Archer, but I don't spot him. The tube train enters the platform—awesome! At least, luck is with me.

I jump on in it, travel another fifteen minutes east, then jump out at the station that is closest to my studio. I head out of the tube, up the quiet street. It's not that late, just past nine p.m. I've been to the studio this late many times before. The wind picks up and the hair on the back of my neck rises. Shit, since that encounter in the subway, I haven't been myself. I need to get over it. Need to live my life. Baron isn't going to be around anymore. I have to accept that. He opted to leave me; I have to learn to live without him.

I hurry my pace, reach the door to the studio, key in my passcode and push open the door. I step in, push the door firmly closed behind me, climb the stairs and reach my studio. Once inside, I lock the door, then head inside the dressing room. I place my handbag on the dressing room table and change into my yoga pants and a sports-bra —good thing I always keep a change of clothes here.

Back in the studio, I choose the track and turn up the volume.

The rhythm from the Maga remix of Eminem's *Ass Like That,* fills the space. I know, I know, not conventional belly dancing music, but I've always eschewed the more classical belly-dancing numbers in favor of an eclectic mix of tunes to which I can really shake my booty.

I shake my hips, bump, grind, stretch again, then launch into the dance. Raise my hands, shimmy, grind-grind-grind, sink to my knees, head down, throw my hair back, spring up. Twirl on my toes, round and round, spread my legs, shake my booty. So, it's not just belly dancing, but a mix of moves I've picked up along the way. A lot of it from watching music videos, classical dancing, taking classes in other different dance forms—salsa, merengue, tango, and other eastern dance forms, like Kathak. Also, ballet—which I'd never been able to master, but which had helped me discipline my moves... Which, combined with the sensuous grace of belly-dancing, helps capture the eye of the person watching and keeps them riveted—at least, so I hope. My heart begins to pump harder, sweat beads my brow, flows down my back. The rhythm picks up and the beats thunder in my veins. I push myself to go faster, slam my feet into the wooden floor, twirl, whirl, pirouette, shimmy—the song ends in a clash of cymbals and I throw myself down, head down, hair in a cloud about my shoulders, my breath coming in gasps. That's when I hear the sound of scuffling. What the—? I jump up as the sound of a thud reaches me.

There's a banging on the door and I freeze.

Who could it be? I reach for my phone and switch off the music. Silence descends. I head for the door, glance through the peephole and freeze.

The man standing there wears a suit. He's staring straight at me. He has a bandage on his forehead. What the—? It's one of the guys who attacked me at the bypass the other day. He stares at the peephole, then raises his fist to bang on the door again.

A small cry bubbles up. I push my knuckles inside my mouth.

I stumble back, grab the phone, go to dial Baron's number, then remember. Shit, I deleted it.

That's when something slams into the door. Shit, he's going to break it down. *Shit, shit, shit.* I dial Isla's number; it goes straight to voice mail. He crashes into the door again and I hear it crack. Fuck, this isn't good. This is not good. I should have heeded Baron's advice and moved my studio somewhere safer, especially after that subway attack. But the rent on this place is so cheap. It's a steal. Now I know why. Clearly, I had left myself wide open and vulnerable. Oh, hell.

I pull up Summer's number; that's when the door crashes open.

The man stomps into the studio, and the phone slips from my hand.

I glance around the space for a weapon, anything that I can use against him. He shakes his head, "Don't even think about it." He stops in front of me and I swallow. *No, no, no, this can't be happening. Why the hell had I given Archer the slip? Why had I not thought this through better? Why had I been so upset with Baron that I had compromised my own safety?*

The guy looks me up and down. "What have we here?" He reaches for me, and I scream. I bring my knee up, kick him in the groin. He doubles over and I rush past him. I am almost at the door, when I feel the weight of his hand on my shoulder. I scream as he kicks my legs out from under me. I fall over, turning my face so my cheek connects with the hard floor, instead of my nose. The breath rushes out of me. Sparks flare behind my eyes. I lay there, stunned, when he grabs my arm and begins to drag me inside toward the dressing room.

I try to yank free, but my shoulder screams in protest. A groan rips out of me. He pulls me toward the dressing room, shoves the door open and throws me inside. I slam into the wall, hit my other shoulder against the hard surface. The pain reverberates down my spine. My head spins. I lose my balance and fall onto the dressing table, which shudders. I slide to the floor and my handbag falls next to me. I snatch it up, hurl it at the intruder. He laughs, even as he catches it, and tosses it over his shoulder.

I lay on the floor as he prowls closer to stand over me.

29

———————

Baron

I am on my way to her house, when my phone rings. I hit the handsfree. "Archer?" I ask.

"Baron, I'm sorry, but she gave me the slip."

"What?" I frown. "What do you mean? Where is she?"

"I'm at her house right now, and she's not here."

I swerve to the side and a car honks angrily as the vehicle passes me by. I hit the brakes and the car screeches to a halt. "What do you mean she's not there? Where could she be?"

"Not sure. Maybe...the studio?"

I release the brakes, peel onto the road, and take a U-turn.

"I'm on my way there now."

"I'm sorry about this. I literally lost sight of her for a few seconds, and she took off."

"We'll talk about that later," I snap. "Just get to the studio."

"On my way."

I disconnect, step on the accelerator and head for her studio. My heart begins to pound; adrenaline laces my blood. "Fuck." I slap my palm on the steering wheel. I knew it; knew I shouldn't have trusted anyone else with the job of watching her. But Archer is good. He is better than me when it comes to surveillance shit. It's why I'd asked him to keep an eye on her. But no one can protect her better than me. No one. And I had been too up my own arse to think clearly. I should have known she wouldn't accept anyone else to watch over her. Shit, if something were to happen to her. No, it's fine. She's fine. She has to be.

Good thing, I am not too far from her studio. In ten minutes, I screech to a halt in front of the building with her studio.

I reach the door that leads to the building, and am about the press the buzzer when a gust of wind blows. The door swings open, then slaps against the frame again. What the—? The hair on the nape of my neck rises. I freeze, pat my side, then swear again. Of course, I don't have a weapon. I am not at war. At least, I thought I wasn't. How wrong I've been. I am in the middle of the biggest fight of my life, the one to protect my woman.

I head for the studio, find the door to the building hanging askew. My pulse thuds at my temples and anger squeezes my guts. I try to take in a breath and my lungs burn. If anyone has dared to hurt her, I'll kill them. The blood pounds in my veins and my heartbeat accelerates. I race up the flight of steps, find the studio door similarly busted. I slip inside. The space is empty except for the purse on the floor.

I jump toward it, look at the contents spread across the floor. Among them is a photograph. I pick it up, glance at the family in the picture. The mother, the father, the older daughter, the younger one with red hair, wearing a red dress. The same red dress I'd seen on the girl in that pub.

My heart begins to race and sweat beads my palms. It's her. I had been right all along. The girl I hadn't been able to get out of mind all these years? It's her. Ava. My Eve. I pocket the photograph when a sound reaches me. I freeze, glance in the direction of the closed door of the dressing room, when a scream rends the air.

My heart slams against my rib cage,

I race across the floor, burst into the dressing room, to find her on the floor.

A man in a suit has her hands pinned back. Another restrains her legs. I take in their features, freeze. They are the same men who attacked her in the subway. What the hell are they doing here? Why are they coming after her?

A third guy, also in a suit, stands over her. He turns to face me and I growl. My vision narrows. Motherfucker, I am going to kill all of them. I lunge forward, grab his shoulders and haul him back. I fling him to the side. He hits the wall at a roll, only to spring up again. I rush toward him, raise my fist, and bury it in his face. His eyes roll back and he slumps.

Before he can hit the ground, I turn back toward the dressing room and freeze. She's on her knees and the man who previously had her hands pinned back now has his arm around her neck. The other guy stands between us.

Both men have their guns pointed on her.

Ava's chin wobbles, her face leached of all color. There's a cut on her forehead, her hair is askew, but otherwise, she looks unhurt. Good.

The man who's standing turns and walks toward me. I throw up my fists and he shakes his head. "Resist and Carlos, here, will not hesitate to shoot your girlfriend."

"Why," I growl, "why would you hurt her?"

"To get back at you, of course." He rocks back on his feet. "You guys need to stop sticking your nose in where you are not needed."

"Let her go," I growl, "she's innocent."

"You should have thought of that before you got involved with her."

A cold sensation stabs at my chest. I'd put her in danger, damn it. I'd thought I was protecting her, but I'd turned the Mafia's attention solely on her.

"She had nothing to do with it," I grate out.

"Oh, but she's such a hot piece of ass. Bet she has a really tight pussy, huh?"

Anger fills my head and my vision bleeds red. I jump toward him, and he raises his gun and fires. I duck and the shot echoes through the space. Ava screams as bits of plaster from the ceiling rain down between us.

"Baron," her voice hitches, "help me."

My heart stutters and the band around my chest tightens.

"Yes, Baron." The man in front of me bares his teeth, "Keep it up and we'll shoot her right in front of you... After we've taken turns fucking her, of course."

"Bastard," I growl, "you'll pay for this."

"Not if we kill you first." He aims his gun at me and I lunge forward again. I grab his arm, twist it. He screams and I watch the gun slip from his grasp to the floor.

He takes advantage of my momentary distraction and buries his other fist in my side.

Pain explodes up my spine and the breath rushes out of me. Bent over at the waist, I don't take my gaze off of her. I hold her eyes. *Stay strong, my love. Don't let them get to you.*

She swallows and tears roll down her cheeks. My guts twist. In that second, I know I'll never allow anything to happen to her. My life was already hers... Now...my heart is too. My soul. Every part of me belongs to her. I won't let these men get to her.

I straighten, turn my gaze on the guy who'd hit me. "That all you got?" I smirk. "Surely you can do better than that?"

His features twist. "I am going to kill you, asshole." The man throws himself at me.

I take the full brunt of his weight, allow my body to go limp as we crash to the floor. We roll away from the dressing room, toward the body of the third guy, who remains unconscious.

The man jumps up, just as I stagger to my feet. He buries his fist in my face. My neck snaps back and Ava screams; blood drips from my mouth. He hits me in the side, and I lurch back. Hits me a third time, and I stumble to the side toward where the gun had slipped from his grasp earlier. I sink down to my haunches and grab the weapon. I train it on him and he instantly throws up his hands. He shifts his gaze from me to his friend who holds Ava captive. The guy turns his gun on me, but Ava screams, "No," and renews her struggles.

Taking advantage of the commotion, the first guy bolts.

I train my gun on the man holding Ava. By now, they are standing, his arm pinning her to his body.

He stares at his friend on the floor, then at me. His hand shakes, as he presses his gun to her temple, "Come closer and I'll shoot her." He swallows. "I mean it."

"Of course, you do." I turn the gun in my hand, hook my forefinger through its ring. "See, I am going to put it down now."

Sweat beads the guy's forehead. I hold up my other hand, palm face up, then bend slowly.

"No tricks," he growls.

I place my gun on the floor, then straighten. "See, that was easy."

"Kick it aside."

I take in his flushed features, the way his hand trembles. Shit, this man is a loose cannon.

"Do it." His voice shakes.

I kick the gun and it skitters to the side.

He bares his teeth, then turns his gun on me. I angle my body to the side but he's already firing. I duck and the shot misses me.

There's a thunk as the bullet embeds in the wall somewhere behind me. He presses down on the trigger again, and there's a clicking sound, and again. Thank fuck, either he's out of bullets or his gun is jammed. I don't care which.

I rush toward him, just as he shoves Ava at me.

I close my arms about her as he brushes past us. He races across the studio floor, out the main doorway.

I pull Ava into my arms. "You're safe." I murmur, "you're safe."

She glances past me and her gaze widens. I turn to find the guy on the ground staggering to his feet.

Shit, I didn't check him for guns. I was too focused on Ava. Fucking fuck.

"Don't do it," I warn as he pulls out his gun. He aims it at us.

Ava freezes in my arms. I release her and she clings to me, "No, Baron, no."

"Let go of me," I snap.

"No, I won't."

"You must."

"I can't."

"You have to."

"Baron, please don't do this. I can't live without you."

"You can." I glance down at her, "Do it for him." *For Edward.*

"No," she shakes her head, "no."

I lower my head toward her, when the sound of a gun being cocked reaches me. I hold her gaze, stare into her beautiful green eyes, swimming with fear, with love.

I love you.

I push her away, then raise my arms.

"Don't come closer," he warns.

I pause, take in the sheen of sweat on his face, the intent gaze, the steadiness of his aim. This guy won't miss. I only hope I can divert him, keep him talking until Archer gets here.

"You don't want to do this," I say in a calm voice.

The intruder's lips twist, "I don't have a choice."

"What do you want, money? I can arrange that for you."

He hesitates.

"How much? A million? 10 million?"

His forehead furrows. I take a step forward, and this time, he doesn't stop me. I make sure to plant my body between him and Ava. *Focus, focus. Keep him talking; keep her covered.*

"You can take everything I have."

His grin broadens. "Oh, but I will." He levels his gun at me, and I draw in a breath. This is it. If I can save her life, it will be worth it.

"No," Ava cries out, "don't do this."

"Shut up," he growls.

I sense Ava stiffen behind me.

"Do as he says," I mutter.

"You stay quiet." He points his gun at me, as I sink to my knees. He aims it at my temple, when the sound of footsteps from the staircase reaches us. The man starts and glances over his shoulder. I lunge for the gun on the floor and fire just as he collapses face down.

Blood oozes out from a wound in his back.

I glance up, take in the man framed by the doorway, holding a gun.

He's dressed in a black T-shirt, a leather jacket and denim jeans. His amber gaze holds mine, his dark hair brushing the collar of his jacket. His features—his very familiar features—are pale. He lowers his gun, glances down at his chest.

I follow his gaze to where blood blooms from the left side of his chest.

"No," I choke out, "no."

I run toward him, reach him as he sinks to his knees. I lower my gun to the floor, then grabbing him, I ease him to the floor.

Footsteps sound, then Ava reaches us. She throws her arms around him, "Edward, oh, my god, Ed!"

To find out what happens next read The Billionaire's Bride HERE

Binge read the Big Bad Billionaire Series

US

UK

All markets

Start the series with Sinclair & Summer's story here

Read Saint & Victoria's story here

Read Weston & Amelie's story here

Read Damian & Julia's story here

Join my newsletter

Claim your FREE contemporary romance book. Click HERE

Claim your FREE paranormal romance book HERE

Follow me on AMAZON

Follow me on BookBub

Follow on Goodreads

Follow me on TikTok

Follow my Pinterest boards

Follow me on FB

Follow me on Instagram

Join my secret Facebook Reader Group; I am dying to meet YOU!

READ MY BOOKS HERE

READ MY BOOKS HERE

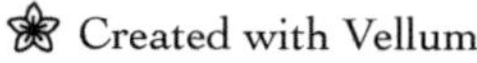 Created with Vellum

www.ingramcontent.com/pod-product-compliance
Lightning Source LLC
Chambersburg PA
CBHW071301190726
48292CB00007B/2645